THE LONG GOOD FRIDAY

Harold Shand 'has made it from Whitechapel to running his own "corporation" and owning his own yacht and classy mistress. He has the police and the local authorities in his pocket, is planning a major London property development and forging links with the international Mafia. Everything indeed is coming up roses for Harold until the Easter weekend when enemies unknown embark on a series of lethal outrages against his organisation. As the story accelerates to a crazy vortex of violence, Harold discovers he has unwittingly crossed enemies whose connections, expertise and dedication to violence outclass his own.'   *Times*

'The first British thriller to even approach the crackling vivacity of the classic Hollywood gangster movies . . . dazzlingly slick.'   *Daily Mail*

'A dizzy switchback of ideas, images and energy. Taking its cue from the metaphysical conundrums of *Performance* and the 70s TV cops capers, it jackknifes the genre into the current climate . . . John Mackenzie (director), Barrie Keeffe (screenwriter) and Barry Hanson (producer) raise myriad issues that are as imaginatively mounted as they are deliberately provocative . . . Wonderful!'   *Time Out*

'A gangster film in the classic old Hollywood mould of sharp craftsmanship.'*Newsweek*

'A refreshing example of how real talent, backed by acting, can freshen a familiar scene and make it spell excitement and significance.'   *Standard*

'Ingenious, imaginative and tremendously exciting.'   *Daily Express*

'*The Long Good Friday* is nothing short of a masterpiece . . . a model of what movies should be and rarely are.'   *Newhouse Newspapers*

The front cover shows Bob Hoskins as Harold Shand. The back cover shows Bob Hoskins as Harold Shand and Dave King as Detective Inspector Parky. All photographs in this volume are reproduced courtesy of Embassy Pictures.

THE LONG
GOOD FRIDAY

BARRIE KEEFFE

METHUEN · LONDON AND NEW YORK

To Barry Hanson

A METHUEN PAPERBACK

First published as a Methuen Paperback original in 1984 by Methuen London Ltd, 11 New Fetter Lane, London EC4P 4EE, and Methuen Inc, 733 Third Avenue, New York, NY 10017.
Copyright © 1984 by Barrie Keeffe

Reproduced, printed and bound in Great Britain by
Hazell Watson & Viney Limited,
Member of the BPCC Group,
Aylesbury, Bucks
Set in 10 point IBM Press Roman by 🅵 Tek-Art, Croydon, Surrey

British Library Cataloguing in Publication Data

Keeffe, Barrie
  The Long Good Friday. – (Methuen screenplays)
  I. Title
  791.43'72 PN1997.L6/

  ISBN 0-413-55550-X

Introduction

The night *The Long Good Friday* eventually got its West End premiere in February 1981, the overflow pipe from the water tank in my attic froze and the kitchen ceiling fell in. If the tank had overflowed five minutes later I'd have been on my way to Leicester Square. Instead of watching the opening credits roll, I was in the attic securing the ball-cock with the tie I'd bought for the occasion and the kitchen was ankle deep in water and floating lumps of ceiling board. The whole story of the film's journey to the cinema screen was a bit like that and so it came as something of a surprise to read in the papers next morning that *The Long Good Friday* had opened — that some new catastrophe hadn't prevented it reaching the screen. Beside the water tank were the two soggy cardboard boxes full of the many abandoned drafts and notebooks charting the meetings and interviews from the initial idea to the 'final version'. It had taken five years.

September 1976
In an Indonesian restaurant on the Fulham Road, a meeting with Barry Hanson to discuss me writing a new TV play for him. He had just produced *Not Quite Cricket* (*Gem* in the theatre) for Thames TV and I had an idea for a sort of comedy about my days as a trainee reporter on a weekly newspaper in East London. Our conversation strayed to the Kray twins, the East End folk-hero gangsters who had been jailed, we realised, exactly ten years previously. Barry wondered what had happened to their old empire during the past decade. Who ran it now, he asked? My first hand knowledge was decidedly skimpy. In the sixties in East London just about everyone you ever met knew someone who had done some job for the Twinnies or had some anecdote to tell of a personal connection. My only 'personal connection' was having once urinated beside the chubby twin in the lavatory of a Bethnal Green pub. I was about 17 and petrified when he (as legendary for his gayness as his violence and unpredictability) invited me to admire something concealed in his trousers. The urinal was swimming before my eyes when eventually, at his persistence, I peered over the porcelain divide to admire not the penis I had tremblingly expected to be shown, but a gun.

Although Barry clearly didn't rate this as a high point for 'our' gangster movie he suddenly decided we were going to make, he revived some useful memories from my trainee reporter days and one did get into the film. I had sped via the number 58 bus to interview a lorry-heister who had been found crucified to the floor of a disused warehouse.

'What happened?' I dutifully asked him. 'A Do-It-Yourself accident, son,' he told me. Back at the office the news editor laughed his head off and told me it was the current favourite punishment for a lorry-heister who evaded paying the percentage of his take to the villains who had not prevented him doing the heist in their manor. So it became the fate of the night-watchman in the film and the scene was pounced upon by one critic, irritated by my screenplay's 'religious overtones which rapidly evolve into full bloodied apocalyptic statements . . . a night watchman is found crucified . . . renewal, resurrection, atonement — all laid on with a trowel, setting the structure of the movie rocking on its foundations.'

This symbolism was not foremost in the minds of either Barry or myself as we finished the meal and agreed that we'd do a gangster film. It would be called *The Last Thriller,* bellowed Barry in his fierce Bradford accent, his arms outstretched, fingers splayed and eyes firmly focused on the cinema hoardings he could suddenly see in the distance behind and to the right of my head. *The Last Thriller* was the first of 87 provisional titles, according to my mildewed notebooks.

24 December 1976
The contract arrived from Thames TV to write a one hour TV film provisionally entitled *The Last Thriller*. Barry has attached a note: 'How are we getting on with it?' The royal *we*.

Spring 1977
To enable *us* to get on with it I set about reacquainting myself with some of the people who had been on my regular journalistic beat in the twilight years of the Krays' reign. Everyone I asked knew what had happened in the past decade: unfortunately everything everyone told me conflicted. The only constant theory was that the Twinnies still ran it from inside, a theory convincingly derided by those who named other names. Hundreds of names, some well-known names from industry, politics and television celebrity. I was told of gang wars and I was told how the whole empire had been agreeably divided up into small areas, each run independently. The tame cop Parky character came out of the one consistency — the idea of the police preferring organised crime to anarchy. 'Calm exterior, no eruptions,' says Parky in the screenplay.

During this time, Barry arranged a series of screenings of gangster movies he thought we ought to see. We watched them in a tiny private screening cinema in Soho on winter afternoons: it was like bunking off school. Quite often the five reels we watched in one showing were from five different movies, French and Italian as well as English and American. Barry's enthusiasm for the project became contagious as he shouted the storyline of the film above the staccato dialogue and machine-gun fire. The sort of film I was to write became clear: it should be the sort of gangster film we'd like to go and see that night. Set in London. Now. The hero would be played by Humphrey Bogart if he'd been born in East London before the war instead of in New York in 1899 (on Christmas Day — no religious symbolism intended). All we needed was a story . . .

Sometimes the luck is with you. I have no note of the date, but I do remember it was snowing the night the storyline for *The Last Thriller* arrived. Outside Tottenham Court Road tube station a man I didn't recognise greeted me like a long lost friend and thanked me for having once been in the magistrates court when he was convicted of an offence which would have caused his family as well as himself great embarrassment had I written it up in the paper. This I hadn't done; I suspected negligence on my part but he had long been convinced that it was down to my compassion for a blatant fit-up. He'd done three months and had stories to tell; our pub crawl ended in North London where a green shirted band sang Irish patriotic songs and ended their set by burning a Union Jack on stage while hats were passed around for pound notes and fivers. Everyone seemed to have an Irish accent. 'This is protection,' said my drinking companion in a whisper as we contributed. The route to the exit was crowded. 'It's protection money.'

How would the Twinnies' successors deal with the IRA *if* the IRA did decide to take them on? The Krays had prospered on terror: the idea of a confrontation between villains using terror for sheer profit in a war with an idealistic terrorist organisation who used terror with greater expertise was suddenly what the film would be about. The hero would be a Thatcher man gone mad — the ultimate self-made capitalist and utterly patriotic. It excited me as an idea because it threw up so many questions; it challenged so many moralities and I wanted to pursue the adventure of a man I might morally detest yet hoped would survive even if I eventually would find myself loathing the qualities that enabled him to endure.

It was an idea so rich with possibilities that I didn't write a word of *The Last Thriller* for two months.

April 1977
Instead I wrote *A Mad World, My Masters,* a modern Jacobean city comedy that
Thomas Middleton might have written (far better) had he been alive in 1977. Joint
Stock had commissioned it and I wrote it during and after an intensive workshop
period. After ten weeks writing, workshopping and rehearsing a comedy the depression
and despair its writer experiences as the play lurches through its first preview defies
description. The audience in the Young Vic not only didn't laugh – they appeared
unaware what they were watching was supposed to be a comedy. The first act seemed
to last several hours. As I slid out of the theatre I expected to find dawn breaking
in the street – instead I found Barry Hanson in the nearest pub, waiting for me,
curious to know how *we* were getting on with *The Last Thriller.*

Good Friday 1977
In a state of euphoria I began our gangster screenplay at seven next morning and
was astonished to find the first draft finished 48 hours later. Thirty eight pages. It was
as though it had come off a teleprinter and although there would be many other
drafts, almost a half of the first version survived through to the text in this book:
the Erroll scene, Parky on the quayside, almost all of Harold's big speeches and the
structure – the swimming baths stabbing, the casino bomb, the explosion of the
Rolls outside the church: Harold's investigation and late realisation of who he was up
against.
      The reason it was set on Good Friday was because I wrote it on Good Friday, to
me always the dullest of bank holidays and immediately beneficial to the story as it
enabled Parky to give Harold time to restore order during a holiday weekend. Every
hour the radio news reported that it was the quietest Easter in Belfast since the present
troubles had begun; I went to the stock car race meeting at Hackney Stadium that
night which is why the stock car race meeting became the setting for the resolution
in the film.
      I delivered the 38-page first draft to Barry's house on Sunday night and on Monday
he said he liked it and would do it.

Autumn 1977
Barry switched jobs; he moved from Thames TV to an outfit called Black Lion Films,
part of the Grade Organisation. He would make two movies for TV and a cinema film.
The Last Thriller would be the cinema film. It would be called *The Paddy Factor*
now. During the autumn the script got longer and longer: Victoria began to talk –
in the first draft she was dumb. By the November draft she had so many speeches
whole new locations turned up: the Royal Opera House and the Festival Hall would be
used as locations since Victoria had become a ballet and opera lover 'culturing' Harold.
Barry dropped the 179-page December draft and said: 'No-one'll hear the singers if
she doesn't shut up'.
      In the next draft Victoria had been to Benenden at the same time as Princess Anne
and this required entirely new Victoria dialogue. Just as Harold was the role
Humphrey Bogart had never played, now Victoria would become the part Lauren
Bacall was born to play had she not been born in New York in 1924.
      In a Golden Egg diner between London and Southend where Barry was TV filming
Bloody Kids, he squirted two sachets of tomato ketchup over a platter of chips and
told me that we weren't writing a mere gangster film: 'This could be a sophisticated
comedy of manners as well.'
      I would find the key to the new Victoria style of dialogue with Harold in Bacall/
Bogart dialogue. The first, unforgettable exchange of dialogue between them in *To
Have and Have Not* would inspire me into the rewrites on draft eight. Since neither of

us could recall that first unforgettable, sparkling exchange, I rented the video. The first line of dialogue Lauren Bacall ever said on screen to Bogart was: 'Can you spare a light?'

While Victoria grew into a speaking part, Harold's status was similarly growing. The first sight of Harold in these drafts was him lording it on his yacht in the St Catherine' dock marina in East London, just east of Tower Bridge. The first impression would be a yacht in St Tropez: when it came to shooting we were refused permission to film the scene there. It was equally difficult to get the amount of information Harold needed to have about the redevelopment of dockland, a heated issue in East London as the fantasy of turning the old derelict docks into a kind-of Torremolinos-on-Thames with redundant dockers becoming holiday camp red-coats for the forthcoming tourist invasion begged Harold's intervention.

We eventually received sufficient data and artists' impressions by posing as potential investing industrialists, which led to the introduction of the Mafia in the shape of Charlie and Tony. This is how Harold would raise the necessary finance and it also increased the inconvenience of the sudden challenge on the very day the Yanks arrived.

By Christmas we had a draft to show an actor. Barry never waivered from his initial casting thought: only Bob Hoskins could play Harold Shand.

January 1978

The first discussion with Bob took place in the London Hospital for Tropical Diseases where Bob would next day give birth to a 27 foot long tape worm he had conceived in Africa while living in a mud hut during the shooting of *Zulu Two*. Barry and I were asked to treat the 'expectant mother' in the usual maternity ward custom – it would not be an easy birth and if the 27 feet of tape worm broke, Bob would have to go through the whole process again.

Bob agreed to play Harold and improvised a few scenes he felt might add excitement to all 'the verbals' and shared his vision of the abattoir scene until his midwife ordered him back to bed. Bob also suggested the title should be *H*. Then the poster could show Harold bloodied and clinging to a huge crucifix sort-of H. He said he'd jot down some ideas and we crept away wishing him all the things all maternity ward visitors say the night before a birth.

The character Jeff was born the day after the tape worm. Hearing Bob's voice delivering some of Harold's lines in the hospital made it suddenly blindingly obvious that Harold must have someone he could really talk to in the film: a kind of son-figure who would one day take over his empire. (*Shand's Kingdom* became a contender for title briefly at this time.) Jeff became an intriguing character for me and Bob took to driving over to my home in Greenwich to share with me sudden, inspired visions he'd seen of who Jeff might be: or rather what Harold might say to Jeff. To get in the right mood Bob sometimes bellowed out Harold speeches he'd memorised in my pub, the Ship and Billet. One night the bar room applauded Bob's impassioned stab at Harold's condemnation for Americans who think they can buy up England.

August 1978

On a sweltering summer night Barry introduced me to the director John Mackenzie in a Greek restaurant in Charlotte Street. I was late and by the time I got there, the band was in full swing, plates were smashing and diners really were dancing on the tables. John had directed two of my favourite pieces of television drama of all time – *Just a Boy's Game* and *Just Another Saturday*. The pandemonium of the restaurant and the oppressive heat made it difficult to talk about his past work: it was as though when we met our discussion of this film was very advanced. John was ankle deep in many drafts scattered beneath the table. He said there was a film here that he wanted to

direct but — this kindly — what I'd written would run for about eight hours. It needed
cutting. Barry, John and I met frequently through the autumn as I filleted the script
until it became 315 pages long.

'Three hundred and fifteen pages,' said Barry one Sunday lunchtime at his house in
Fulham.

That was the draft without the Glyndebourne scene, I mentioned.

'Do we need Glyndebourne?' asked Barry. John asked a lot of questions,
challenging every moment in the story, every motivation.

'In the middle we could do with a massive explosion,' he said. Later the explosion
in the middle occurred at Harold's favourite old pub that he had 'rescued from the
redevelopers': a whole Dickensian pub exterior and interior was built on the Isle of
Dogs to be blown up — and so effective was the building that our count-down to the
explosion was hurriedly halted three times as passers-by stepped into it to buy a pint.

Autumn 1978
Barry said it was on, we'd been given the green light. It would be made in the summer
of 1979. After each meeting with John and Barry and often Bob, I re-wrote parts of
the script: since each new draft averaged 150 pages, we now had knee high piles of
paper to wade through whenever we met.

The function of the Jeff character became clearer during the autumn. John was
now running each draft through his mind as though watching a movie. He felt there
should be a big, climactic scene between Harold and Jeff that would be verbally
dramatic before the visually dramatic stock car scenes. Jeff would be the Judas. The
cat-and-mouse scene would end in Jeff's death. Once this scene was written, hundreds
of sheets of paper could be ripped up, but by now for every sheet that vanished,
another appeared. We needed a title and John was adamant that he would not direct a
film called *H, Harold's Kingdom, The Last Thriller,* or *The Paddy Factor.* He wouldn't
even pay to watch a film with one of those titles.

I feel embarrassed flicking through the notebook of titles that we discarded: *Havoc,
Diabolical Liberty, Citadel of Blood,* even. I spent a night hunting titles in the Book of
Psalms. Every time we thought we had hit on the right title, it turned out that
someone else had already used it.

Easter 1979
On Easter Monday Black Lion Films moved into a suite of unfurnished offices above a
boutique specialising in second-hand American fifties clothes at the southern end of
Carnaby Street. Barry summoned me to his office that afternoon; it was the only
office with a desk and a chair. He said: 'We are now in a pre-production situation.'

All the other rooms were vast and bare and painted white and had unconnected
telephones. 'Choose any one,' said Barry. 'It will be your office.'

In the next office — a vast bare room with an unconnected telephone — John
had neatly laid out every draft of the screenplays page by page so that they covered
the floor.

'The script,' he told me, 'is about five hundred pages too long. There's enough
script here to make a runway for a Concorde.'

'The first shot of Harold — he steps off Concorde.' said Barry.

The definitive screenplay would be written in this very room: Barry and John
would be in constant attendance to ensure that when I cut the script it got shorter
instead of longer.

Shooting would begin in July and last eight weeks. We would spend the weeks until
shooting began finalising the script. Bob arrived unexpectedly and announced that he

had no engagements and would be able to devote all his time to the three of us as I 'bashed out the shooting screenplay'.

Summer 1979
The weeks that followed were the happiest working weeks of my life. The offices began to fill with people as well as furniture; a designer, cameramen, technicians joined the pay-roll and casting got under way as I worked away on the typewriter wih Bob, Barry and John at my shoulder page by page. This meant that not a line got through to the final screenplay unless we all agreed.

Two weeks before shooting began Bob suggested Black Lion Films sent him to Greece to get a suntan and get in shape for the film 'running up and down mountains'. John, Barry and I endured the London heatwave and read the postcards Bob sent with further 'visions'; the suggestion that Harold's mother become Greek Orthodox instead of Roman Catholic was rejected.

The first scene filmed was the yacht party to welcome Charlie. The filming ended after nine weeks on a Sunday morning in Bethnal Green Town Hall with a scene between Harold and Councillor Harris which finished up on the cutting room floor.

Hasty rewrites had been required during the shooting for all sorts of reasons – the day of Harold's big speech as the yacht sailed under Tower Bridge had to be changed because of the unprecedented tornado which blitzed the Fastnet race so tragically and caused our vessel's captain to return to port hurriedly.

An end of shooting party was held on the Sunday night in a hotel overlooking the marina in which we had been refused permission to film.

'*The Long Good Friday* is in the can,' said John, who had chosen that title out of desperation as a working title the day before shooting began. It was just a working title until we found the right one.

The Long Good Friday had been my daily, obsessive preoccupation for three years and so that party was a strangely sad occasion.

For Barry and me, it was the end of our first film, but for Barry it was just the end of round one. *The Long Good Friday* would never have reached the cinema had he not fought for it over the next 18 months with a courage and energy that astonished me. Instead it would have been savagely cut up, with all references to the IRA removed, and shown on television in March 1981.

May 1980
The film came close to being selected as the official British entry at the Cannes Film Festival. Alexander Walker wrote in the *Standard,* London: 'I can only think it was because of the film's freakish example of right wing Toryism gone to the bad which must have appealed to the cynical French film selectors . . . Hoskins tearing a strip off his craven hearted American partners who back out as the IRA comes in and at the same time boasting of Britain's Common Market membership as an alternative entrée into criminal profitability might have made even Margaret Thatcher blush if she had heard the answering jeers from the French audience.'

Barry had rushed the incompletely edited cut to Cannes for the screening. In London Jack Gill, chairman of Black Lion Films, had ordered the butchering of the film into TV acceptability.

The next public screening was at the Edinburgh Festival Film Festival in September 1980. To get the film there required Barry 'taking possession' of the cutting copy and hiding it in the boot of his car; both Barry and the cutting copy were hunted for a fortnight as the hired editor waited in a Soho office to make the cuts Mr Gill required. The joke around Wardour Street at this time came from the often seen 'Jack Gill presents' opening credit: 'Jack Gill resents to present,' even joined the graffiti on the walls of Soho pub lavatories.

23 August 1980
The Long Good Friday was shown at the Edinburgh International Film Festival. A tribute was organised for John who was born and raised in Edinburgh and it was planned to screen five of his pieces (originally six for showing). It was agreed that *The Long Good Friday* would be shown and at the reception at the Caledonian Hotel, John was invited to speak about his work. He used the occasion to bang the drum for *The Long Good Friday* to a roomful of journalists who had just returned from a screening of it.

Next day Ned Chaillet wrote in the *Times* 'Bets are already being laid that it will win its star Bob Hoskins an Academy Award nomination.'

Derek Malcolm in the *Guardian: 'The Long Good Friday* is apparently threatened with cauterisation for the television screen instead of a cinema showing. Lord Grade who put up the money will have to think again.'

The critical approval did nothing to lessen Gill's determination to chop up the film: the Grade block-buster *Raise the Titanic* was being less appreciated than *The Long Good Friday* which cost a tiny proportion of the *Titanic*'s vast budget.

The London Film Festival loomed ahead as *The Long Good Friday* hit another problem.

The *Guardian: 'The Long Good Friday* has run into trouble over the dubbing of a version for American television. Apparently the company involved, a subsidiary of Lord Grade's ITC, was worried that Bob Hoskins would not be intelligible to American viewers. So his voice has been replaced by another actor.'

Bob took out a High Court injunction to prevent the distribution of the American version.

13 November 1980
Our film remained intact for the London Film Festival. In the *Times,* David Robinson thought the screening at the National Film Theatre was 'a stirring affirmation that there is still vast talent in British commercial film making'. He also wrote, 'The producers have decided to consign it to television. In terms of corporate accountancy (and the film business today is much more the preserve of accountants than showmen) television is the safe and sensible short-term choice. If the film goes straight onto television (through ACC's subsidiary Associated Television) two thirds of the £1.1 million costs will be immediately written off against the advertising revenues (excess profits) levy paid by the television companies. (Ironically, in fact, in a country where state support for cinema has always been so reluctant, television can derive an indirect sort of subsidy for film production in the form of such sums set off against the Treasury levy.) Foreign sales would readily cover the balance of the film's cost ... whatever one's sympathy with the accountants, however, in terms of the film, the public and the British cinema at large, it is a frightful loss if the film goes on television.'

John made a speech after the screening in which he clarified absolutely his feelings about Jack Gill. It received more applause than the film. Bob shocked me with the news that the dubbed version had been dubbed for America by a British actor with a Midlands accent: the reason he was suing was because he rightly felt the dubbing behind his back was 'a prostitution of my acting ability'. Our jubilation at the undeniably triumphant reception was killed when Barry quietly passed to us the news he now had: the bastardised *The Long Good Friday* would be transmitted on 24 March 1981 and there could be no general release for it. There was no party. We met in the old Carnaby Street office a few nights later to discuss what we might do if indeed there was anything more that could be done.

The Carnaby Street offices were in the process of being closed down. A Salvation Army brass band was practising carols on the pavement outside. We sat in the dark and in silence, noticing that the fight Barry had been staging was showing: he looked ill. Bob had just bought a poodle and it sat on his lap while he muttered darkly that he knew a 'geezer who'd do the necessary for a grand. That's only 250 quid each.' he said stroking the poodle.

I found it hard to imagine how the TV version could make any sense at all if what was to be cut was actually cut: there would be no mention of the IRA, Jeff would not be killed and any suggestion at the end that the IRA could not be defeated (this, illogically in a version that did not mention the IRA in the first place) would be erased 'as an example to young people'.

John pressurised Jack Gill relentlessly, as did Barry who argued in the press for its cinema showing thus: the film had been specifically constructed for the cinema and all the contracts had been negotiated under a movie, not a TV, agreement. ITC, he said, had 'reneged' on a tacit agreement to give the film a theatrical run for its money following a special screening for Lord Grade who had given every indication of liking it.

Three days before Christmas the Grade Organisation bowed to the pressure and offered to sell the film outright (apart from the UK commercial TV rights which it would retain) for the price it had cost Black Lion to make.

That cost was put as two thirds of two million dollars: thus began a last race against the clock to find a buyer who would release it theatrically as the March 24 transmission neared. ACC's quoted reason to sell the film was that *The Long Good Friday* was 'uncommercial'.

January 1981
Bob met Eric Idle at a party and suggested Handmade Films might like to buy *The Long Good Friday*. Handmade had previously rescued Monty Python's *The Life of Brian* when Lord Grade's brother Bernard Delfont 'pulled out because he found it too controversial' (*Standard*).

Barry and John came round the night of the deadline for the sale of the film. Just before the deadline, news arrived that Handmade had bought *The Long Good Friday*. By then the wine had already been drunk and the pubs and off licences were closed.

February 1981
On Thursday 26 it opened simultaneously at the Ritz, Leicester Square, the Classic, Oxford Street and the ABC cinemas in Fulham and Edgware Roads. It equalled the Ritz box office record take in its first week.

March 1981
The *Sunday Mirror* splashed a story headlined 'The great video fiddle – buy a hit movie for £12' and went on to describe how touts in Leicester Square were selling bootleg videos as well as tickets for *The Long Good Friday*. The film was now on general release throughout Britain.

March 1982
The New York premiere. *US* magazine wrote: 'With *The Long Good Friday* Bob Hoskins immediately joins the movies' most illustrious rogues gallery, a criminal roster that includes Edward G. Robinson's Little Caesar, James Cagney's Public Enemy, Rod Steiger's Al Capone and Micky Rooney's Baby Face Nelson.

Bob laughed when he read the review in a cab.

'It doesn't mention if that was the dubbed version,' he said. Then he added: 'It must have been the uncommercial version.'

New Year's Eve 1983
At a New Year's Eve party at John's — some talk about the bootleg videos Barry, John, Bob and myself had all been offered since the film opened. And discussions about what looks like a real possibility of the money being raised for the sequel we all want to make. We've got the story, and Bob will play Harold Shand again. Barry will produce it with John directing. The four of us reunited. Every one of us would tell the story of the making of *The Long Good Friday* in a different way, from a different focus. No doubt it'll be the same with the sequel; but I think I can say this for the four of us — it is hoped *The Long Good Friday II* will have a less traumatic journey to the cinema screen.

Barrie Keeffe, 1984.

THE LONG
GOOD FRIDAY

The Long Good Friday is a Calendar production for Black Lion Films Ltd. It went on general release in Great Britain in 1981, and in the USA in 1982. The cast is as follows:

HAROLD SHAND	Bob Hoskins
VICTORIA	Helen Mirren
CHARLIE	Eddie Constantine
PARKY	Dave King
HARRIS	Bryan Marshall
GUS	George Coulouris
JEFF	Derek Thompson
MAC	Bruce Alexander
ERROLL	Paul Barber
1ST IRISHMAN	Pierce Brosnan
ERIC	Charles Cork
PETE	Bill Cornelius
TONY	Stephen Davis
PRIEST	Alan Devlin
PHIL	Leo Dolan
KID	Dexter Fletcher
JACK	Alan Ford
COLIN	Paul Freeman
ALAN	Brian Hall
HAROLD'S MOTHER	Ruby Head
DAVID	Karl Howman
DAVE	Nigel Humphries
GINGER	Paul Kember
MAN UNDER CAR	Trevor Laird
CAROL	Patti Love
PRETTY IRISH YOUTH	Kevin McNally
BOSTON	Bill Moody
RAZORS	P.H. Moriarty
2ND IRISHMAN	Daragh O'Malley
DON	Dave Ould
EUGENE	Georgie Phillips
CHEF	Olivier Pierre
O'FLAHERTY	Tony Rohr
BILLY	Nick Stringer
SHERRY	Kim Taylforth
JIMMY	Robert Walker
FLYNN	Robert Hamilton
ELDERLY SWIMMING BATH ATTENDANT	Brian Hayes
COMMISSIONAIRE	James Ottaway
MAN IN ERROLL's KITCHEN	Trevor Ward
SAVOY HOTEL CLERK	James Wynn

Music composed by Francis Monkman
Associate Producer Chris Griffin
Editor Mike Taylor
Director of Photography Phil Meheux
Produced by Barry Hanson
Directed by John Mackenzie

1. Exterior. Countryside. Night.

In the first light of dawn a rambling, white-washed old farmhouse, half-hidden by trees in an otherwise bleak landscape. We see the house in its eerie isolation from a distance. It may have been abandoned long ago.

2. Exterior. The window. Night.

The leaded window of a downstairs room of the farmhouse fills the screen. Two men in their thirties sit at a table waiting: one smokes, the other man stares vaguely at an orange shaded table lamp in the surprisingly well-furnished room. Just the amber glow of the lamp illuminating the room. All this in silence.

3. Exterior. Quayside. Day.

The sound of a vessel's horn. Early morning light. An elegantly dressed man in a black suit and white sweater descends a gangplank from the ship which has just docked. We dwell on the expensive looking black leather suitcase he is carry-ing. At first we don't see his face – just the suitcase in his hand. He crosses the quay and gets into a waiting saloon car. As the car moves off, he opens the case. Beneath a scattering of clothes, he peels away a false lining to reveal enough neatly-bound bundles of fifty pound bank notes to fill three briefcases. He removes two, closes the lid of the case and slides the money into the inside pocket of his jacket. Now we see his face. He is Colin. He smiles from the back seat, checking that the driver in front of him has not seen his action.

4. Exterior. Main street. Day.

From a low elevation, we see the saloon pull to a halt at the kerbside of a busy, but run-down city main street. It is cold and rubbish blows about in the wind. We see the outline of a man waiting for Colin, who gets out of the car, crosses

the pavement and hands the stranger the suitcase. The man, whose face we cannot see, walks away briskly as Colin returns to the saloon which immediately drives off.

5. Interior. Pub bar. Night.

The crowded, smoke-filled bar of a large Victorian pub. Vast gin palace mirrors, well worn red velvet seating and crumbling plaster. The only woman in the place, it seems, is the barmaid. Colin goes to the bar for a refill for himself and Phil, the driver of the saloon. As Colin leans closer to the barmaid to make himself heard above the juke-box, his eyes meet the eyes of a pretty youth sitting alone at the far end of the bar.

Close up of the youth, half-smiling at Colin.

Colin's face up close, inhaling on his cigarette, then smiling at the youth. He tilts his glass towards him. The youth looks coy and then he sips at his Guinness and grins at Colin across the bar.

6. Exterior. Countryside. Day.

The same long shot of the farmhouse in the stark countryside. Now the sun is rising.

7. Exterior. The window. Day.

One of the two waiting men rises as the stranger comes into the room and places the suitcase on the table. It is hastily opened, the clothes discarded and the false bottom removed. The bundles of bank notes are tipped onto the table and the three men prepare to count them. None of them speak.

8. Interior. Pub bar. Night.

Now Colin is sitting in a corner beside the pretty youth. Phil, the driver, gathers their glasses to buy another round. Alone

*with the youth, Colin smiles and begins
to stroke the youth's thigh. They speak
but the sound of the juke box prevents us
hearing what they say. Colin moves
closer to the youth, laughing. He places
an arm around his neck and whispers into
his ear as his other hand continues to
caress the youth's thigh.*

9. Interior. The window. Day.

*Some agitation among the three who have
been counting the money. Clearly it is
less than anticipated. They retrieve the
suitcase to check for another concealed
hiding place when, suddenly, the window
panes are smashed by a uniformed man
with a machine-gun. Other uniformed
men burst into the room with guns. In a
daze the three money-counters raise their
hands in surrender. No words are spoken.*

10. Interior. Pub. Night.

*The bar is more crowded, and noisier.
Colin and the youth, their arms around
each other, are moving towards the exit
with Phil, who looks uncomfortable. As
they reach the exit, Colin remembers
he wants more cigarettes. As he returns
to the bar, Phil and the youth go out into
the pub's car park.*

11. Exterior. Pub car park. Night.

*As the driver and the youth reach the car,
three hooded men dash towards them
from a nearby parked truck. Wielding
coshes they bundle their terrified victims
into the saloon and immediately drive
them out of the dimly-lit car park, with
blazing headlights and screeching tyres.
Colin wanders out from the pub and is
confused and worried to find the saloon
gone.*

12. Exterior. Country lane. Night.

*The saloon approaches us through the
darkness and stops at a lay-by. The*

*hooded men drag from the rear seats the
driver and the youth – now corpses.
They carry them to a ditch hidden from
the road and dump them in it. We see
their bodies unmoving in the mud of the
ditch in the light of the saloon's headlights as it drives away into the darkness.*

13. Interior. Euston Station. Day.

*The public address system announces the
arrival of a train from Liverpool and from
the roof of the station we focus on the
removal of a coffin from the guard's
compartment of the recently arrived
train. The guard stands on the platform
watching the undertakers gently carry
the cheap coffin to a waiting hearse: he
respectfully removes his ridiculous
uniform hat. As the coffin is slid into the
hearse, we pick out the face of the black-
clad young widow, Carol, who stands
watching beside a relative in a dark
overcoat. She wears a veil and looks pale
and utterly bewildered. She gets into the
relative's car and they follow the hearse
out of the station.*

14. Exterior. Italian Restaurant. Day.

*At first we see the pavement tables of
this smart, evidently expensive restaurant
through the soaking windscreen of a Rolls
Royce. Razors, a middle-aged man dressed
like a merchant banker with a face on
which a military moustache and stitch-
scars incongruously jostle for prominence,
is cleaning the windscreen of the rolls
waiting for Jeff who is dining al fresco
across this busy West End street with
Councillor Harris.*

    *They are at the end of their meal.
While Jeff studies the plans, Harris
constantly gulps at his brandy. Jeff is
younger than the councillor.*

JEFF. Harold'll be well pleased.

    *Jeff rolls up the plans and fastens
them with an elastic band. Harris is
conscious that Jeff has again spotted
him gulping alcohol.*

HARRIS. When's he back?

JEFF. Today.

HARRIS (*worried at having handed over the plans Jeff is casually pocketing*). Highly confidential. I need them tomorrow Jeff, for a council meeting.

JEFF. Don't worry. (*He laughs at Harris's anxiety.*) I'll get them photocopied. You'll have them back on time.

HARRIS. What about the Americans?

Jeff enjoys Harris's unconcealed concern.

JEFF. I reckon they're coming.

HARRIS. Good.

Harris stands and adjusts the combination lock of his briefcase.

About the nosh . . . on the Corporation?

He makes an insincere gesture to reach for his wallet.

JEFF. 'Course, councillor.

HARRIS. See you, Jeff.

JEFF. See you.

Jeff signals for the bill as Harris hurries to his estate car. As Jeff begins to sign the check brought by the waiter, we see behind him the hearse and the funeral cars we saw at Euston Station pulling to a halt. Out of the relatives' car comes Carol. She strides towards Jeff and as we close on her face she removes her widow's black veil and spits at Jeff's face. Immediately she returns to the car.

JEFF. Wait a minute!

He wipes away the spittle and turns to see the funeral procession depart. As the relatives' car passes in front of us we zoom in on Razors' face across the street: he is polishing the window of the Rolls – but his eyes tell us he has witnessed Carol's action.

15. Exterior. Heathrow. Day.

Dramatically and spectacularly, a Concorde coming in to land.

16. Interior. Heathrow terminal three foyer. Day.

Looking at the Concorde passengers coming into the foyer: we close in on Harold. He looks impressive and takes the focus from all the other travellers. Jeff greets him and they hug like a son with his long-lost father.

17. Interior. Rolls Royce. Day.

Jeff and Harold side by side in the back seat of the Rolls as it cruises out of Heathrow and begins the motorway journey to London.
Harold is glancing at the architectural plans on his lap.

JEFF. He needs the plans back by this afternoon.

HAROLD. Good old George. (*A direct look at Jeff.*) Everything all right while I was away . . . ?

JEFF. Yeah. (*He thinks. Looks at Harold, wondering what he means.*) The new casino's gone through.

HAROLD. No problems?

JEFF. No, everything's all right.

HAROLD. Here, did anyone guess where I was?

JEFF (*unable to resist the joke*). There was a rumour about a health farm.

They both laugh. Harold pats his stomach.

One or two mentioned, maybe, New York.

HAROLD. But nobody guessed?

JEFF. No.

18. Exterior. The marina. Day.

A church bell is ringing mournfully as we look down on the new yachting marina built beside the Tower of London – the redundant docklands have now been converted into a lush Costa-del-Sol-like pleasure centre. Brilliant spring sunshine. We pan across the sailing centre and the river – it might be St Tropez. We close in on the largest and most expensive-looking vessel. Harold's Rolls Royce draws up to the gangplank and we now pick out Harold's mother being helped by Victoria down the gangplank from the deck of the yacht to the quayside.

MOTHER. I should have left ten minutes ago. I'll be late – I hate being late for church.

Victoria helps Mother into the Rolls. As it drives off out of the marina Victoria waves, smiling. When the car is out of sight, Victoria sneers.

VICTORIA. Have a nice Easter – God rot your soul.

19. Exterior. Deck of the yacht. Day.

Harold enjoying the sun, sipping at a drink as Victoria arrives at his side.

VICTORIA. Oh Christ, Harold – she's always worse when she's going to church.

Harold laughs and touches Victoria's waist.

HAROLD. My mother's got very religious in her old age, ain't she? Church three times today. It's Good Friday.

He raises the jug of drink, offering to pour one for Victoria.

Another Bloody Mary?

Victoria sits on the chair beside him. Sailing boats pass and the sun makes the crystal glasses sparkle.

VICTORIA. She thinks Paula's an angel and I'm the devil in disguise.

HAROLD. O, well – me and Paula only got divorced ten years ago. Give mother a chance to get used to it.

VICTORIA. Cheers. (*She accepts the glass from Harold and sips.*)

HAROLD. Cheers. You organised everything?

VICTORIA (*lighting a cigarette, putting on sun glasses and relaxing briefly*). It's all coming along. Charlie should be landing about now . . . (*Looking at Harold.*) Maybe we should have gone to the airport to meet him.

HAROLD. No, no, no. Play it cool. When the governor of Coca Cola drops into London, the Queen don't go rushing off to Heathrow –

VICTORIA. The Queen?

HAROLD. You know what I mean. And play all that up. How you went to school with Princess Anne, played hockey with her, all that.

VICTORIA. It was lacrosse at Benenden. Hockey's frightfully vulgar. (*This in a mock cut-glass accent.*)

HAROLD (*squeezing her hand, happy*). Yeah, yeah, plenty of that.

Victoria helps Harold fix the cufflink he's fiddling with.

The Yanks *love* snobbery. They really feel they've arrived in England if the upper classes treat them like shit.

VICTORIA. Gives them a sense of history? (*She's obviously quoting one of Harold's favourite sayings.*)

HAROLD. Yeah.

She gets out of the chair, deposits her unfinished drink and briefly kisses Harold's forehead.

VICTORIA. I'd better check how the chef's progressing.

HAROLD. Here, that geezer don't arf know about grub. The smells that have been coming up from the galley all morning have been driving me potty.

Victoria smiles affectionately as she goes towards the stairway to the lower deck. She turns back to watch Harold begin to pour himself another drink from the jug.

VICTORIA. You lay off the vodka. Oi!

Harold watches her go, blowing her a kiss. Then he refills his glass when she's out of sight.

20. Interior. Yacht galley. Day.

Frantic activity. The meal is being prepared by a number of assistants to the chef who wears spotless white uniform and chef's hat — and remonstrates with Victoria, almost juggling with the plates.

VICTORIA. Ça va?

CHEF. O, madame, regardais-moi ça . . . Je demanderais blanc. Mais ils sont bleus avec les friezes —

VICTORIA (*calming him*). Alors, c'est trés agréeable, nous vous remercions beaucoup.

From the doorway of the galley, which we now see is full of enormous vases of flowers which the hired florists are arranging, we see Alan and Razors watching the carryings-on from outside.

21. Exterior. Galley. Day.

Alan and Razors both look uncomfortable in starched collars and their best suits.

RAZORS. That chef's a right horrible ponce.

ALAN. Yeah, well — he's French, ain't he.

Razors nods, sipping from a beer can — But implying he is not satisfied with Alan's explanation.

22. Interior. Yacht dining-room. Day.

Victoria squeezes the chef's hand, having placated him and as the chef returns to the galley Jeff enters: He watches her inspect the beautifully laid table; masses of flowers on the lace cloth, the crystal glasses and cutlery all sparkling.

JEFF. Very nice. (*He breathes in the smell from the galley.*) These French geezers really know their stuff, eh?

Victoria carries a plate to the sideboard which is loaded with the cheeses. She replaces the plate with another.

JEFF. That new?

VICTORIA. Bought them yesterday. Twenty quid apiece.

JEFF. I bet Harold was reluctant to take the labels off.

VICTORIA. He broke two of them demonstrating their exquisite delicacy.

Their eyes meet. They are standing very close together.

He doesn't know his own strength.

Jeff avoids her eyes by going to the cheeses. He dips a finger into the garlic butter and licks it.

Have you sorted out immigration for the Yanks?

JEFF. Yeah, Parky's dealt with all that.

VICTORIA. Then you may go and have a drink on deck.

Jeff grinningly acknowledges that she is treating him in the way a headmistress might deal with a backward but promising pupil.

23. Exterior. Church. Day.

From a high window of the Catholic church, we watch the Rolls Royce being reversed into a convenient position in the car park. When it stops, we close in on Harold's chauffeur. He gets out of the car apparently impatient at the length of the Good Friday Mass taking place inside the church. We can just hear the service. He lights a cigarette and checks his watch.

24. Interior. Church. Day.

As sunlight streams through the stained glass windows, we peer down the nave of the church towards the altar where the congregation are forming a queue to kiss the base of the large crucifix being held by scarlet-cassocked altar boys.

Close up of Harold's mother as she kneels before the crucifix, making the sign of the cross, and bends forward to kiss the base of the crucifix.

As she does this, we travel up the crucifix noting the figure of Christ with outstretched arms.

Mix to:

25. Interior. Swimming baths. Day.

Colin atop the highest diving-board, his arms outstretched as he prepares to make a spectacular dive. We follow his journey into the water and watch him climb out of the pool at the far end. The modern swimming bath is almost deserted, but as Colin walks back to the diving boards we notice the admiring look from a boyish, dark-haired youth. We also notice a pot-bellied man behind him. When Colin pushes back his hair before climbing the diving board again and looks up to smile at the youth, who smiles back, he does not notice the pot-bellied man. Colin smiles at the youth in a way that reminds us of how he smiled at the young man in the pub previously.

26. Exterior. Yacht deck. Day.

The deck is crowded with Harold's admirers in their best clothes, drinking champagne which waiters serve constantly. Harold, now wearing a tie and jacket, mingles with his guests, greeting them. Music plays. We are reminded that the yacht is not moored in St Tropez at all – the deserted warehouses in the background tell us we are actually in the redundant London docks.

HAROLD' Hello, mate. Having a good time? Enjoy yourselves.

As Harold shakes hands with this guest and his wife, he moves towards Councillor Harris who gulps at the champagne as though come tomorrow there might not be any left.

Councillor, Harris – those plans came in very handy, my son. Much obliged.

HARRIS. No sweat, Harold.

Harold puts his arm round Harris's shoulders, leading him out of earshot of the other guests.

HAROLD. The licence on me casino – that go through all right? No problems?

HARRIS. A slight one.

HAROLD. What's that?

HARRIS. Councillor Taylor seems to think you're a gangster –

HAROLD. Leave off! (*He laughs at the preposterousness of the idea.*)

HARRIS. What's the s.p. on the Americans?

HAROLD. Well, just pump them full of information, everything you've got. You know?

HARRIS. Right. Instant planning permission, all that sort of chat.

HAROLD. Yeah, plenty of verbal.

HARRIS. Right.

HAROLD. Well, the Yanks think we're a cack-handed corner shop over here, you know what I mean. Exude efficiency, right?

HARRIS. Yeah, right. I'll tell them how quickly my little enterprises are springing up, that should appeal. (*He drains his glass.*)

HAROLD. Yeah, terrific, terrific.

Harold slaps his back and moves towards Parky and Dave, under the deck canopy. Victoria stands between them: Parky twice as old as Dave.

Parky – you're not drinking!

PARKY. Harold, you know I only drink when I'm on duty.

HAROLD. How's business, all right?

PARKY. Yeah, only a drizzle of complaints!

HAROLD. Get a lot of that in your game, eh? Hello, Dave!

DAVE. Hello, Mr Shand. (*They shake hands.*)

HAROLD. How are you? Last time I saw you, you had spots . . .

DAVE. Oh, thanks very much! Even I notice the coppers are getting younger now.

VICTORIA. He's a Detective Sergeant, now, Harold.

HAROLD. Is he? Celebration — Oi, come here.

He takes a bottle of champagne from a passing waiter and refills their four glasses.

Champagne, my son. Here's to you. (*He clinks Dave's glass.*)

VICTORIA. Nice to see real friends doing well. Here's to real friends. (*She raises her glass and the three men clink glasses.*)

HAROLD.
VICTORIA. } Real friends
PARKY.
DAVE.

Jeff has arrived. He coughs to get Harold's attention.

HAROLD. Oh, Jeff — won't be a minute.

Jeff and Harold move through the crowd of guests. Almost all of them are middle-aged. One elderly man wears a mayoral chain of office.

27. Interior. Harold's study on the yacht. Day.

Harold closes the door, leading Jeff in. Reproductions of Victorian nautical paintings in heavy gilt frames fill the walls. The wall behind Harold's enormous desk, however, is decorated with naval swords and cutlasses.

HAROLD. Keep your eyes on the boys' behaviour, will you? I don't want any of them acting like delinquents.

JEFF. No chance, they know it's important. I told them to put their wedding suits on.

HAROLD (*he smiles*). I think you're going to like Charlie. So — what's the plan?

They are now standing by a detailed model of the River Thames, from the Tower of London to East Ham — as envisaged by an artist in its ideal state, like a Costa Brava resort.

JEFF. A cocktail here, so he can clock the marina, then off down the river so he can see the scope of the whole project.

HAROLD. Terrific. Have you fixed the mooring?

JEFF. Yeah, it's all under control.

HAROLD. Another thing: Harris has got a lot of talking to do this afternoon. So keep him off the booze — top him up with Perrier water or something.

JEFF. Sure, of course.

Victoria comes into the study.

VICTORIA. Harold — he's here.

Harold and Victoria smile at each other with delight.

HAROLD. All right, you two pipe him aboard and I'll be right up.

Victoria and Jeff go out onto the deck leaving Harold to stare at the dream the model promises. A vessel's horn sounds outside.

28. Exterior. Yacht deck. Day.

Against a stunning river view of Tower Bridge, Harold and Charlie embrace each other on the bow of the now moving yacht.

HAROLD. I can't believe you're here. You, the kid from New Jersey.

CHARLIE. The boy from Stepney.

Victoria arrives with a white jacketed waiter carrying a tray of champagne. She hands a glass to Harold and another to the older Charlie.

VICTORIA. Charlie, have some champagne.

CHARLIE. Victoria, you should be the captain of this boat. Great timing.

They all laugh: so does Tony, younger than Harold and wearing a white suit. Harold thinks he's another waiter.

HAROLD. I want to propose a toast. Hands across the ocean.

CHARLIE. To the future, Harold. (*They clink glasses.*)

HAROLD. To the future here, yeah.

CHARLIE. Harold, I don't think you met Tony when you were in New York.

Tony smiles and steps nearer.

HAROLD. Tony who?

CHARLIE. Tony Giovanci, my lawyer. Harold – Tony.

TONY (*shaking hands*). Very nice to meet you, Mr Shand.

Victoria senses Harold's unease and so links arms with both Tony and Charlie.

VICTORIA. Let me introduce you to some people. They're important but they're nice.

They go to mingle with the crowd leaving Harold alone with Jeff.

HAROLD. You'd better keep your eye on that Tony. Charlie never said he was going to bring anyone.

JEFF. They always come in twos, like the bailiffs. It means they mean business.

Harold is obviously relieved at this: he laughs heartily and slaps Jeff on the back and they join everyone else.

29. Interior. Swimming baths. Day.

Colin in the water swimming towards the deep end where the boyish, dark-haired youth sits. As Colin reaches the edge of the pool, the youth looks directly at him and encourages Colin to follow him. Colin watches the youth go into the changing rooms, then climbs out of the pool and follows.

30. Interior. Shower room. Day.

We pick out Colin gingerly approaching the showers through the steam of the shower room. Colin leans against the open door cubicle and smiles. From Colin's point of view we see the youth, naked beneath the shower, turning to smile back at Colin. Now we see Colin from the youth's point of view and we also see the pot-bellied man appearing out of the steam, dagger in hand, behind Colin's back. Colin embraces the youth who pulls a kitchen knife from its hiding-place behind the shower curtains and plunges it into Colin's stomach. Behind Colin, the pot-bellied man stabs the dagger repeatedly into Colin's back. As Colin slumps to the floor, we see the knife wounds seeping blood.

31. Interior. Church foyer. Day.

The increasingly impatient chauffeur peers through the foyer window into the nave of the church, smoking his cigarette.

32. Interior. Altar of the church. Day.

From the chauffeur's point of view we see the priest at the altar. We pick out Harold's mother, looking emotional.

PRIEST. The lamb of God that takes away the sins of the world. Happy are they who are called to his supper.

CONGREGATION:
PRIEST. Lord, I am not worthy to receive you. But only say the word and I shall –

33. Interior. Church Foyer. Day.

The chauffeur checks his watch and, grunting to himself goes out of the church. We hear the prayer continuing.

34. Exterior. Day. Church.

Still hearing the prayer, we watch the chauffeur go to the Rolls Royce which is parked directly outside the church doors. He gets in. As he closes the car door, there is a massive explosion and the Rolls is engulfed in an inferno.
In the silence following the explosion we hear applause. The applause is coming from the gathering of guests on Harold's yacht:

35. Exterior. Yacht deck. Day.

The screen outlined by Tower Bridge as the yacht cruises away from it, centre of the river. Harold's head fills the screen.

HAROLD. Ladies and gentlemen. I'm not a politician — I'm a business man . . . with a sense of history. And I'm also a Londoner . . . And today is a day of great historical significance for London.
Our country's not an island anymore — we're a leading European state. And I believe . . . that this is the decade in which London *will* become Europe's capital, having cleared away the out-dated.

We pan across the assembled guests facing Harold. They are all nodding serious agreement. Parky sits at a table and behind him stand men who are clearly leading lights in Harold's heavy mob. Tony stands between Councillor Harris and Jeff, as interested in Harold's audience as in his speech.

We've got mile after mile and acre after acre of land for our future prosperity. No other city in the world has got right in its centre such an opportunity for profitable progress.

We close in on Tony, flanked by

Harris and Jeff, who smiles towards Victoria, whom we now see is standing close to Harold with Charlie at her side. She hands Charlie a glass. We are moving downriver from Tower Bridge now: other famous London landmarks can now be seen against the sky.

So it's important the right people mastermind the new London. Proven people, with nerve, knowledge and expertise.

A quick cut from Harold to Alan and Razors who exchange a brief glance.

And that is why you are all here today. All trusted friends. And why Charlie and Tony are here today . . . our American friends. To endorse the global nature of this venture. Let's hear it, ladies and gentlemen . . . Hands across the ocean.

Harold raises his glass for the toast. From his point of view, his entire audience joining in the toast.

EVERYONE. Hands across the ocean.

36. Exterior. River Thames. Day.

The yacht travelling through East London towards Tilbury. Some of the guests are dancing on the upper deck. A small jazz band plays.

37. Exterior. Yacht. Day.

Harold pauses outside Charlie's cabin. Charlie leans on the rail. He watches a huge cargo vessel docked in the George V, being unloaded. Harold stands beside Charlie, breathing in the river air.

HAROLD. There used to be eighty or ninety ships in this dock at one time. They used to queue up to get in.

Harold waves vaguely towards the cargo vessel they are passing. Charlie takes more interest in Harold's facial expression — his emotion — than the ship.

All the way from Galleon's Reach,

right the way down to Tilbury. This used to be the greatest docks in the world. At one time. This did.

CHARLIE. Things change, Harold. Don't get nostalgic. Look to the future. Remember, you're thirty-five minutes from Europe here. Great potential.

He playfully punches Harold, who now notices how tired Charlie is.

CHARLIE. I live in a new country and I respect the past. But at the same time, I always keep my eye on the future.

Harold considers this, waiting for the significance to register. Charlie slaps Harold's shoulder and pushes open the door to his cabin.

38. Interior. Charlie's cabin. Day.

Charlie coming in, sees a ship hand about to open his briefcase on the bed – the final job in unpacking all Charlie's baggage.

CHARLIE. Don't touch. I'll take care of that.

Charlie stares at the ship hand who nods and goes. Harold leans casually in the doorway. He watches Charlie inspect the cabin.

HAROLD. You have a good sleep, Charlie. We've got a tight schedule. I've got my property lawyers all lined up for you to meet. The best, the very best. Then there's this accountant geezer I've lined up who specialises in gambling tax —

Charlie's face up close. For the first time we see how hard he is.

CHARLIE. This isn't a horse race, Harold. Don't rush me.

Harold reacting to this. Charlie smiles.

CHARLIE. I hate tight schedules, Harold. I'll get everything covered that I have to get covered. But in my own time.

The two men stare at each other in the

sudden silence. *Harold might say something, but Victoria suddenly emerges in the doorway beside him. She smiles brightly.*

VICTORIA. We're just docking now. It'll be nice and quiet if you want to sleep, Charlie. Come on Harold, let's leave him alone for a while . . .

Harold nods, smiles blandly and goes out, closing the door. Charlie, alone, looks at the hat the steward had left on his bed. He picks it up and strokes it.

CHARLIE. Bad luck, putting a hat on a bed.

39. Exterior. Passageway on yacht. Day.

Victoria hugs Harold outside Charlie's cabin to reassure him. Harold gnaws his fist, as the riverside becomes increasingly depressing – deserted warehouses and derelict buildings.

VICTORIA. Relax, he'll be all right.

HAROLD (*suddenly bright*). Yeah. Poor old sod, he's probably got jet lag.

They both laugh.

40. Exterior. The river. Day.

We sweep along the river and watch the yacht dock in a bleak, depressing dock on the Isle of Dogs. This empty city landscape is unnaturally quiet and unmoving – everything is still.

41. Interior. Harold's study on yacht. Day.

Through the porthole we watch the guests disembarking, getting into their cars and driving off. Parky and Dave are the last to go, waving and staggering slightly. During this, a telephone is ringing.
Now up close on Harold's hand as he lifts the receiver. He has been watching his guests depart, the yacht now moored.

HAROLD. Yeah, yeah — what? What?

Harold's face seems to go rigid. He is holding a whisky glass. His grip on it tightens and the glass is crushed. He replaces the receiver and looks at Jeff and Razors who stare at him, alarmed at whatever news has so obviously distressed and angered Harold. Harold growls.

HAROLD. This is . . . a diabolical liberty.

Harold paces in front of his desk.

JEFF. What is?

HAROLD (*shouting*): Blown up! He's dead. Eric is dead. A car bomb.

Harold glares at Jeff.

JEFF. A?

HAROLD. Mother's all right. Suffering from shock, she's in the hospital.

JEFF. I don't understand?

HAROLD. You'd need a million dollar computer to understand this. Who'd do such a thing? It's outrageous. Outside a church! (*This a bellow.*) You don't go crucifying people outside a church, not on a Good Friday.

Jeff and Razors both look scared at Harold's outrage. They're relieved when Victoria comes into the study, uneasy at Harold's ranting.

VICTORIA. What's the matter, Harold?

HAROLD. Eric's been blown up.

Victoria registers this.

VICTORIA. A bomb?

JEFF. Yeah, in the Roller.

VICTORIA. I don't believe it. When?

HAROLD. Just now. Mother's in hospital, suffering from shock. I'm not surprised, she went to church to say her prayers, not to get blown up.

Harold stares out of the window.

JEFF. But why?

VICTORIA. Is someone trying to discredit you in front of . . .

HAROLD. What — the Yanks? No, no, no. Nobody knew, did they?

VICTORIA. Well, they mustn't find out.

JEFF. No, they're sleeping.

HAROLD. Right, I want everybody in the Corporation working on this fast. Right, and I want Colin here, where is he?

RAZORS. He went swimming.

HAROLD. Swimming? He should have been *here*. Right, I want everybody working. Jeff, you get on the blower. Razors, you round them all up and you get them moving — fast. Right. Keep them on their toes, 'cause I want this settled. Tonight.

VICTORIA. And you better see your mother.

Harold slows down. Jeff and Razors about to go.

HAROLD. Yeah. Listen. If anyone hears anything, anything at all, I'll be at the Mayfair casino, right? It's the work of a maniac. I'll have his carcass dripping blood by midnight . . .

Harold's face up close: the menace.

42. Exterior. Quayside. Day.

Harold is getting into the Jaguar on the quay beside the moored yacht. As Jeff is about to get in, a big Ford screeches to a halt. Jeff goes and speaks to the agitated driver — one of the gang. Harold's face up close through the window of the Jag, watching. Jeff approaches Harold.

JEFF. More bad news. Colin.

HAROLD. Colin?

JEFF. Yeah . . . dead.

Harold is open-mouthed. Jeff gets into the Jag and they drive off.

43. Interior. Swimming baths, changing room. Day.

Harold stares down at Colin's naked, blood-stained body as the water in which it lies in the foot-bath gurgles away. The elderly attendant scans Harold's face for a sign of emotion.

44. Interior. Swimming baths. Day.

Harold stands beside the swimming pool, clutching the rail. When he speaks, his voice echoes around the deserted baths as though he were making a memorial service oratory in an empty church. Jeff, Razors and the pool attendant stand to one side.

HAROLD. I did my National Service with Colin. We did six months in the glass-house together. Two kids of eighteen. Six months. Put us right through it, the bastards. Salisbury Plain manoeuvres. We used to have to hump this bleeding great wireless about. One winter . . . snows, blizzards, freezing the bollocks off the wild ponies . . . I got lost. In them days, you stayed lost until they nicked you for being AWOL. And Colin on a 24-hour pass. He came out looking for me on his own . . . Was lucky he found me, I would have froze to death . . .

JEFF. Yeah.

HAROLD. Colin never hurt a fly. (*Razors and Jeff exchange a glance.*) Well . . . only if it was necessary. Was always clean, weren't it? Was never nothing malicious about Colin.

RAZORS. Why slice him up?

HAROLD. Mind my grief!

RAZORS. Sorry, H.

HAROLD. Me and Colin was very close. I'd known him since I was at school. What's going on? They try and blow up me mum, wipe out me best mates . . . What they trying to do? Put the frighteners on me, wind me up — what?

The grandad-like pool attendant is beside Harold now. He speaks confidentially.

ATTENDANT. Harold, to keep it all incognito, they're going to collect the body in an ice-cream van.

HAROLD. There's a lot of dignity in that, ain't there? Going out like a Raspberry Ripple.

ATTENDANT. They're going to store the body in the freezer down the abatoir.

HAROLD. All right, Grandad, thanks for the call. Did anyone see anything?

ATTENDANT. Not what happened. The pool attendant found him but I told her it was an haemorrhage.

HAROLD. Good lad.

ATTENDANT. We had to close the baths, Harold.

HAROLD. Now open them up. Let them enjoy the holiday. If you hear anything, anything at all, you give me a bell, right?

He hands the attendant a £50 note and hugs him in a matey way. Then briskly to Jeff and Razors.

HAROLD. Come on.

45. Exterior. Casino. Day.

The Jag turns into a Mayfair side street and as it halts outside the casino, Eugene, the manager, runs to greet Harold the minute he gets out of the car.

EUGENE. Thank Christ you're here.

They cross the pavement and go towards the casino entrance.

JEFF. Any news?

EUGENE. Eh?

HAROLD. Colin's murdered.

EUGENE. Colin's what?

JEFF. Dead.

EUGENE. Where?

HAROLD. In the swimming pool.

EUGENE. Drowned?

HAROLD. Don't be stupid, he did life-saving.

EUGENE. Well, what's it all mean, a bomb in here and —

HAROLD. You what? (*Stunned at this.*)

EUGENE. Well, there's a bomb in the casino . . .

RAZORS. You better show us.

46. Interior. Mayfair casino. Day.

Close up of the briefcase alarm-clock bomb on a gaming table. We pull back as Harold approaches it.

HAROLD. I wonder how it got disconnected?

EUGENE. Well, a wire must have come loose when Lil opened it.

HAROLD. Stroke of luck, though, weren't it? . . . Last night. Were there any peculiarities?

EUGENE. Usual crowd . . . regular punters . . . nothing really.

HAROLD. What, no strangers?

EUGENE. Few Arabs . . . A good night, nothing unusual.

HAROLD. 'Nothing unusual' he says. Eric's been blown to smithereens, Colin's been carved up and I've got a bomb in me casino and you say nothing unusual!

EUGENE. You know what I mean, Harold.

Jeff comes in, curious.

JEFF. Parky, meeting, King George V dock, now. He's put out a story the bomb in the car was a gas leak, buy us some time.

HAROLD. Nice one. Come here (*He takes Jeff to one side.*) . . . There was nothing unusual when I was in New York, was there?

JEFF. No, nothing at all.

HAROLD. What, nothing alien?

JEFF. No.

HAROLD. How much did we pay Parky last year? Twenty grand?

JEFF. More.

HAROLD. Right. Then he can start earning his bloody money.

Harold's point of view: the bomb.

47. Interior. Jaguar. Day.

From Harold's point of view looking out through the windscreen as it cruises down an East End main street. Harold sits in the front beside Razors who drives. Jeff sits in the back. Now we see Harold's confused face.

HAROLD. Who's having a go at me? Can you think of anybody who might have an old score to settle or something?

Razors is chewing gum and he shrugs.

RAZORS. Who's big enough to take you on?

Jeff watches Harold's reaction.

HAROLD. There used to be a few.

RAZORS. Like who?

HAROLD. Yeah, they're all dead.

48. Exterior. King George V Dock. Day.

The Jaguar speeds through the dock gates and pulls to a halt in a huge storage shed in the unused dock. We dwell on the gutted wreck of the bombed Rolls Royce as Parky comes away from it to greet Harold.

PARKY. Let's walk.

Harold and Parky walk together alongside the water's edge in the deserted acres of Dockside. The Jaguar follows at a discreet distance.

Now, we can't have bombs going off,

Harold. Can't have corpses. I had to stick my neck right out to keep this out of the hands of the forensic blokes.

HAROLD. You come up with anything?

PARKY. Nothing. I thought you were going to tell me.

HAROLD. What — no whispers?

PARKY. Not a thing . . . Look at this place . . . D'you know, I once caught the pox off some Indonesian bird here? I was just a bobby on the beat, then. So, this is where they were going to build the 1988 Olympic Stadium. Can you imagine nig-nogs doing the long-jump along these quays?

The Jaguar is moving slowly behind them. Harold waves it ahead.

HAROLD. Stick a rocket up their arsehole, they'll jump all right . . . I want action on this, Parky.

PARKY. Well, the Yanks are clean, we checked them out.

HAROLD. No, you've got to go down to a third division messenger to even come up with a sniff of villainy with that lot. What about Tottenham?

PARKY. They can't even nick car batteries without getting electrocuted.

HAROLD. Some of the Clancy mob are out . . .

PARKY. No, this is too . . . er, accomplished for them. Besides, no one's had their teeth pulled out.

HAROLD. Spades?

PARKY. Do they overlap?

HAROLD. Never dealt in narcotics . . . How do I know — don't know what they're after, do I?

PARKY. I'll check it out . . . I'm sorry about Colin.

HAROLD. Yeah. I've put him on the missing persons list, that should hold it off for a while.

PARKY. It's just as well. The commissioner'll be poking around.

HAROLD. Well, stall him. I should have this sorted out by this afternoon. I'm hoping . . .

The Jaguar waits just ahead of them and Razors hands Harold a brandy flask. Harold fills the cap and hands it to Parky and swigs from the flask himself.

PARKY. Been looking forward to this deal of yours, Harold, with the Yanks. The legitimisation of your corporation. I don't like fuss . . . calm exteriors. Now, ten years there's been no aggro and it's all been down to you, Harold. You've had it under control. Now do yourself a favour — get this lot under control before the heavy mob's on you like a ton of hot horse shit.

Harold reaches into the car again.

HAROLD. Here, give us that case. Here, get that checked out. will you? (*He hands Parky the briefcase.*)

PARKY. What is it?

HAROLD. It's the bomb from the casino.

Alarmed, Parky holds the case away from himself.

PARKY. You been riding around with a bleeding bomb?

HAROLD. It's all right, it's been disconnected.

PARKY. Oh . . . I'll get the bomb people to have a look at it.

HAROLD. No, Parky, get it checked out privately, right?

PARKY. Cheers.

Close up of Harold's face.

HAROLD. I want the name of your top grass.

PARKY. He trusts me, Harold.

HAROLD. I can get more out of him than you can.

PARKY. That's true.

HAROLD. You do realise just how much

this deal's going to be worth in 1988, do you? Billions. I'll cut you in for a percentage . . . for the name of your grass.

PARKY. He trusts me, Harold.

HAROLD. I trust you.

PARKY. I've known him a lot of years –

HAROLD. Then you should remember his name, shouldn't you?

PARKY. If I give it to you –

HAROLD. No 'ifs', Parky.

Parky considers the offer.

PARKY. A percentage?

Harold nods.

PARKY. Erroll. (*He drains the cap, gives it to Harold and strides off with the briefcase.*)

HAROLD. Erroll The Ponce from Brixton . . . You can't trust anybody.

He peers at Jeff through the open car window.

Did you two hear that?

RAZORS. Yeah.

HAROLD. Brixton, come on.

He gets into the Jaguar.

49. Exterior. Brixton side street. Day.

A young black works under a jacked up old Cortina. Reggae music is playing loudly from a portable cassette beside him. The Jaguar slowly comes to a halt beside the mechanic. Harold lowers the window and peers down at him.

HAROLD. Oi, which is Erroll's house?

The mechanic looks up from under the car.

MECHANIC. Never heard of him, mate.

HAROLD. Razors . . . a little bit of respect here I think.

Razors gets out of the Jaguar and slowly and deliberately kicks away the jack, causing the Cortina to fall. The

mechanic rolls out of danger and yells.

MECHANIC. Fucking hell, what you doing? You crazy?

HAROLD. I don't like people looking up my nose when I'm talking to them.

MECHANIC. You could have fucking killed me.

HAROLD. Way things are going today I'd probably have got you a cut price funeral. Now, Erroll's house. Which one is it?

MECHANIC. Number 33.

The street from Harold's point of view. People are sitting on steps leading to house front doors, all staring at him.

HAROLD. This used to be a nice street, decent families, no scum.

Razors gets back into the driving seat and they move on down the street, through a passage of staring black youths.

50. Interior. Erroll's house. Day.

The bedroom door bursts open. Razors enters holding a gun, Harold and Jeff close behind. Erroll is in bed with his arms around a white girl. Both are naked.

HAROLD. Beauty and the Beast. Blow his head off.

Razors holds the gun close to Erroll's ear.

ERROLL. Hey . . .

HAROLD. You in training or you doing this for pleasure?

ERROLL. We had a party last night . . .

HAROLD. Booze, bints . . . and pox.

ERROLL. Harold, get him to take that metal out of my earhole . . .

HAROLD. No, I'm disgusted . . . Shoot him, let's put some muck on the ceiling.

ERROLL. Please . . . what do you want?

HAROLD. You seen anything of my Eric flying past your window about two hours ago?

ERROLL. What are you talking about?

HAROLD. Come on, downstairs. Down in the kitchen with you, my son . . . I want verbals with you. And put some deodorant on, I'm heavily into personal protection.

Whilst Razors and Jeff take the still naked Erroll out of the room, Harold looks around. He stops, picks up a syringe, looks at the girl.

Filth. Is there no decency in this disgusting world? Here . . . While he's with us — give yourself another prick.

51. Interior. Erroll's kitchen. Day.

Erroll stands naked by the sink, his hands covering his genitals. Harold opens the fridge door and takes out a bowl of peeled prawns.

HAROLD. Tell him what your name is.

RAZORS. Razors.

Harold stands alongside Razors eating the prawns while Razors removes his jacket. Then he opens his shirt to reveal massive, ugly, scars.

HAROLD. Otherwise known as Clapham Junction. Or — as the youth of today call him — the Human Spyrograph.

Harold picks up a cleaver.

RAZORS. Sixty-five inches of stitching . . . Now you're going to feel what it's like, boy.

HAROLD. And he was a very popular fellow.

Erroll's fearful face up close.

ERROLL. Look, Harold, what do you want?

Harold hands the cleaver to Razors.

HAROLD. Well. I have it from a very reliable source that you know what's

what, that you have ears — and I want to know what you've heard.

ERROLL. Look . . . am I supposed to know something?

HAROLD. Razors . . .

Razors slices Erroll across both buttocks. Erroll screams, clutching the sink.

What do you know about Colin?

ERROLL. What about Colin? I don't know nothing about Colin . . . Look, Harold, I've been here all night . . . Look, what's up?

HAROLD. Someone's been playing Guy Fawkes with my Rolls and a touch of Jaws in the lido, that's what's up, mate. What about Eric?

ERROLL. Eric?

HAROLD. You heard.

ERROLL. Well, he doesn't like Colin . . . I mean, queers get right up his hooter, you know?

HAROLD. After what happened this morning, you'd have to find his hooter to get up it.

ERROLL. Eh? Something up with him, then?

HAROLD. Well, let's put it this way. Apart from his arsehole being about fifty yards from his brains and the choirboys playing hunt the thimble for the rest of him, he ain't too happy.

ERROLL. Well, I haven't heard nothing —

HAROLD. Well use your Scouse ears . . . Listen, Erroll. The only decent grass is the grass that grasses to me, right?

ERROLL. Harold . . . if I knew something —

HAROLD. Colin's been stabbed!

ERROLL. Well . . . his boyfriend used to come here to score, but . . . but he never said nothing, so I know nothing. . . . I mean . . . a lot of people come here to score, but . . . We sell very good shit – (*Increasingly scared.*)

HAROLD. What – like you? Who's got it in for me?

ERROLL. I don't know.

HAROLD. Cut him.

Razors slices Erroll's buttocks; Erroll screams.

I still can't hear anything . . .

Razors slices again.

ERROLL. I don't fucking know!

Erroll breaks down, sobbing. Harold's face up close looking manic. Then he calms and leaves with Razors and an anxious-looking Jeff.

52. Exterior. Erroll's house. Day.

Harold, Jeff and Razors coming down the steps of the house as three white kids of about 13 wait beside the Jaguar.

KID. Minded your car, mister.

HAROLD. Should've asked for the money first.

KID. Could have slashed the tyres . . .

Harold laughs and gives the kid a pound note.

HAROLD. There you are. Go and get drunk.

RAZORS. Little acorns.

HAROLD. Eh?

RAZORS. From little acorns grow . . .

HAROLD. Exactly. That's how I started.

RAZORS. Didn't we all.

HAROLD. Not Jeff . . . Busy getting himself an education, weren't you?

JEFF. Ah, different generation, that's all.

They get in the car, Jeff in the back.

HAROLD. Billiard halls was my game . . . Remember old Sammy? Sammy? I tore up two of his tables in a week. He used to pay me *not* to play . . . What do you think?

RAZORS. Look, you told the Yanks you controlled it here. If they're sticking – how many millions in? Perhaps they want to check you really do control it.

HAROLD. . . . No, no, that's way off the mark, leave off. They might check books and finances but they're not going to start wiping out me firm, are they? They don't want anarchy.

53. Exterior. Brixton side street. Day.

Harold's point of view through the windscreen as they cruise along the street.

HAROLD. These people deserve something better than this.

His view of a mother and children in tatty clothes sitting on house steps: decaying image.

Better than dog shit on the doorstep.

54. Exterior. Yacht. Evening.

Sunset over the river and through the window of the yacht's dining-room we see elegantly dressed Victoria handing drinks to Tony and Charlie with Harris standing beside the seated Americans. They are smiling and relaxed.

55. Interior. Harold's study on the yacht. Evening.

Harold urinating in his study's lavatory, leaning out of the doorway to face Alan and Dave.

HAROLD. So nothing?

ALAN. Not a word – well, no one's heard.

HAROLD. No one's heard nothing? That just ain't natural. Like one of them silent, deadly farts . . . no clues and then pow, you go cross-eyed.

The sound of the lavatory cistern flushing as Harold steps into the study tugging the zipper of his trousers.

DAVE. Well, we've asked all the usual —

HAROLD. Well, maybe it's about time you asked the unusual, ain't it?

ALAN. Well, like who? All the chaps are out asking, H.

HAROLD. What — you given up? Where are they?

ALAN. Down the casino.

HAROLD. Well, get them off their arses and make them start again, right? Go on, what are you waiting for?

ALAN. Right.

They exchange glances and leave. Jeff enters from another door.

HAROLD. We heard from Parky?

JEFF. Not yet. Eugene'll 'phone the minute he checks in. Razors is back with the car.

HAROLD. A?

He goes to the study bar and pours himself a massive scotch.

JEFF. Dinner at the pub.

HAROLD (*he had forgotten this*). O, Christ. (*He downs the drink.*)

JEFF. You've got to entertain them a bit, after all, haven't you . . .

HAROLD. Yeah. (*He slams down his glass.*)

56. Interior. Yacht dining-room. Day.

Harold has switched on a confident smile as he comes in to the gathering looking at the river sunset at the stern end of the dining-room. Harold wears an evening suit and Victoria puts her arm through his. Jeff hovers in the background. Charlie, Tony and Harris remain seated.

HAROLD. You all refreshed then?

CHARLIE. You bet. Now I'm ready for your tightest schedule.

HAROLD. Like you said, Charlie — this ain't no horse race. Let's relax tonight, eh?

CHARLIE. Sorry to hear your bad news, Harold.

Harold darts a glance at Victoria.

TONY. Victoria was just telling us all about it.

VICTORIA. Well, she hasn't been well for a long time, has she Harold . . . ? Your poor mother.

Harold almost visibly sighs with relief.

HAROLD. Don't worry, she'll be all right. She's a fighter. Know what I mean? But I had to spend some time with her, you understand.

CHARLIE. That's nice, Harold.

VICTORIA (*winding a stole around her shoulders*). Well, shall we go? I'm dressed and ready for dinner.

HAROLD. It's my favourite pub, You're going to love it.

He squeezes Victoria's hand in gratitude as he leads Charlie out.

57. Exterior. Quayside. Evening.

Harold leads Charlie down the gangplank to the waiting cars as the others follow. The river glows with the setting sunlight.

HAROLD. I bought this pub about two years ago, Charlie. To stop the big breweries turning it into a slum. It's got Charles Dickens links, historical — very 'olde London'. You'll love it.

Victoria is in Jaguar's driving seat as Harold gets in. Charlie, Tony and Razors get in the rear seats. Jeff and Harris go to the open top Mercedes.

JEFF. I'll drive the councillor in the Merc.

HARRIS. God help me.

He turns to Harold for moral support as everyone laughs.

You're laughing — you haven't seen him drive!

JEFF. You can always walk, sunshine.

The cars head into the sunset.

58. Exterior. Riverside pub. Evening.

From a distance we see the ancient pub against the river sunset. We close in on a window of the upper level.

59. Interior. Riverside pub. Evening.

The small and exquisite a la carte restaurant overlooking the river. The main table is being laid for an elaborate meal. A sense of exclusiveness. A pair of waiters are adding final touches to the table arrangement as we pan across the room: the river sunset, the flowers and the old framed prints lining the walls, and through the patio windows we see the Jaguar approaching at a distance, followed by the Mercedes.

60. Exterior. Riverside pub. Evening.

From a low elevation, we approach the pub in the Jaguar. Just before we reach it there is an enormous explosion in the upper level: the pub seems to be ripped apart. We shudder to a sudden halt as flames and smoke cloud our view.

61. Interior. Jaguar. Evening.

Harold's face aghast through the windscreen of the Jaguar, then Victoria's beside him as debris and shattered glass hit the Jaguar's bonnet.

62. Exterior. Riverside pub. Evening.

Screams and shouts from the pub as Harold leaps out of the Jaguar followed by a horrified Victoria. Charlie and Tony stand behind them watching the evacuation of the injured from the pub. Jeff takes charge while Harris hovers.

JEFF. Charlie, Tony — stay back. It might still be dangerous. Stay back.

Harold and Victoria now help the injured as ambulance sirens approach: smoke still billows from the pub.
Harold looks up at the staggering

pub manager Pete, his face and clothes blackened by the blast.

HAROLD. You all right, Pete?

PETE. I'm all right, H.

They look at the casualties on the pavement.

HAROLD. Any customers still in there?

PETE. I think they're all right downstairs. It blew up there in the restaurant.

From Harold and Victoria's point of view: the devastation through the glassless window of the restaurant on the upper level.

VICTORIA. Jesus. If we'd been five minutes earlier . . .

HAROLD (*he looks at her*). Yeah . . .

RAZORS. Keep them there, Jeff. It's a lot safer.

JEFF. Right.

Razors runs to Harold, who stares in disbelief at the havoc.

HAROLD. Shit.

RAZORS. What the fuck is happening?

HAROLD. Help Pete.

Razors goes to Pete who is supervising the carrying out of the injured.

Victoria, occupy the Yanks. Do anything that's necessary — just buy me some time.

VICTORIA. OK. I'll take them to dinner at Justines.

HAROLD. Terrific.

VICTORIA. Get Razors to phone for a table.

Harold speaks to Razors as Victoria goes to Charlie and Tony standing by the Jaguar with Jeff.
She tries to laugh it off.

It was a gas leak.

CHARLIE. Gas?

VICTORIA. It's this new natural gas we have now. It causes dangerous leaks sometimes. Harold's dealing with it and he wants us to go on to a restaurant and he'll join us later. (*She looks at Jeff.*) I'll drive − stay with Harold, will you . . .

Jeff watches them get in the car with Harris. As they move off a police car arrives with sirens sounding, followed by a fire engine.

63. Interior. Pub restaurant. Evening.

Pete and Razors are operating fire extinguishers to douse the fires in the blackened room.

PETE. I thought that French cook was taking a lot of trouble but this is ridiculous.

Outside we can hear police warnings through a megaphone to keep well back.
    Jeff and Harold come up the stairs and through the smouldering doorway. Harold angrily kicks a table.

HAROLD. How the fuck did they get in here in the first place?

He accuses Pete with his eyes.

PETE. Leave off H, you know how many people come up here to use the loos and that −

HAROLD. And nobody spotted nothing, nothing at all?

PETE. Nothing happened this evening, mate.

They look at darkness descending over the river outside.

Mind you, a few days ago two guys came here. They wanted to offer protection. I thought they were comedians − big hats, sunglasses . . . I thought the agency had sent them here for the cabaret.

HAROLD. Protection? From *my* boozer? They actually made threats?

PETE. Yeah, well . . . I told them to piss off. I took no notice of them.

HAROLD. Much obliged.

PETE. Look, I'm sorry mate. You know, I didn't want to worry you like . . .

He looks at Harold. Harold scares him.

I'm sorry.

HAROLD. Razors, come here.

Pete eases away as Harold instructs Razors.

I want all the Corporation at the Mayfair casino in half an hour. Right?

Razors nods.

Get on the trumpet right away and tell them I want them all there and I don't want no excuses. I'm going to nail these bastards, right?

RAZORS. You don't know who they are . . .

Razors begins to descend the stairs but stops as a length of ceiling timber beam crashes to the floor beside Harold. Harold's eyes flash in the smoke of the smouldering beam at his feet.

HAROLD. But we're going to find out, ain't we? It's getting dark. People get frightened in the dark. And so they talk, don't they!

Parky arrives at the top of the stairs as Razors goes.

Hello, Parky. I'm afraid the dinner got a little bit burned.

Harold smiles savagely and waves an arm at the destroyed restaurant. He grabs Pete.

Well, what did they look like − these comedians?

PETE. I don't know, H. I never seen them before. They just looked like any other Micks. Stupid, heavy Micks.

HAROLD. Micks?

PETE. You know, Irish. Right hard-looking Paddies.

In the far end of the restaurant, through the smoke we see Jeff look up

*from his fire fighting. He stares at
Harold who doesn't notice him.*

I never dreamed they'd do this, I'm
sorry.

*Harold releases him and stomps to
Parky.*

PARKY. Harold . . .

They descend into the bar below.

64. Interior. Riverside pub. Evening.

*The devastation in the bar seems even
worse. Firemen are active and the whole
place is smoking. Harold and Parky stand
amid the ruins.*

PARKY. Irish, he said Irish. This is
Special Branch, Harold. This ain't
normal villainy.

HAROLD. It's indecently abnormal. That
up there was meant for me.

*Jeff loiters behind them on the
stairway as Harold and Parky go out of
the pub into the street. Jeff follows,
glancing at the extent of the damage.*

65. Exterior. Riverside pub. Evening.

*The ambulancemen are attending the
injured and a crowd has gathered. Parky
looks around and then says to Harold:*

PARKY. This is fucking serious.

HAROLD (*suddenly cold*): I'll tell you
what you should do. Check out all the
Micks. Any heavy mob who are
working on my manor. I want names
and addresses.

*Harold strides towards the Mercedes
with Jeff. Parky runs after him and
grabs Harold's lapel but quickly
releases it.*

PARKY. Will you listen to what I'm
trying to tell you? This is very serious.

HAROLD. Leave off Parky. Just villains
trying to frighten their way into a
few quid.

PARKY. Harold we are talking about

bombs. Two bleeding bombs today.

HAROLD. Have you got the casino one
checked out yet, by the way?

PARKY. I'm still waiting for the lab
report.

HAROLD. Well, get a fucking move on.

*Harold gets in the car beside Jeff
and slams the door.*

PARKY (*almost pleading*). Harold, if
that bomb is Irish − it's a different
game. Those boyos don't know the
rules.

Harold laughs. Then he glares at Parky.

HAROLD. Names and addresses of the
Micks here, right?

*Jeff revs the engine and they speed
away from Parky who stands shaking
his head. He is in an almost visible
cold sweat.*

66. Interior. Mayfair casino. Night.

*The gathering of the Corporation in the
dimly lit sanctity of the gaming-room.
The chandeliers and crimson drapery
resemble a church and this a religious
service as Harold stands at the far end
of the roulette table that dominates the
room. We move slowly towards him,
picking out the faces of the men who wait
for him to speak. When we reach Harold
we see the collection of armoury on the
table in front of him − pistols, machine-
guns and ammunition. Razors and Jeff
stand either side of him facing the gang.*

HAROLD. Two or three Micks have
been very busy covering a lot of
ground since yesterday and not one of
you lot has turned up with a thing. It
is impossible that no one knows
nothing. Someone, somewhere knows.
Right?

*The gang from Harold's point of view.
Silence.*

And now, tonight, we are going to
find the person who knows, right? I
want a top catcher from every manor

and I don't want no punters, right. This is personal. I am taking this personally. I want the man who knows. So who fancies what?

Harold shuffles the guns.

ALAN. Me and Chris'll take Soho. We'll go and see Maltese Ricky – a couple of drinks and he'll talk.

Harold slides a revolver to Alan.

HAROLD. Use that. It's cheaper. And remember, the licence is in the post.

Alan pockets the revolver while everyone laughs.

ALAN. Yeah, well – I only use it to scare the pigeons off me caravan roof, don't I?

Everyone laughs again and Harold freezes the merriment.

HAROLD. I don't want none of you playing Roy Rodgers with this lot, got it? Soon as you've finished with them – they go back to Razors.

Razors nods his approval at the correctness of this procedure.

DAVE. What about the Finsbury Park Hillbillies?

HAROLD. I like a singsong but who do you fancy for a lullabye?

He slides another revolver towards Dave and awaits expectantly.

JACK. Chopper's in the boob.

DAVE. What about Harry and Pinchers?

JACK. Both of them?

HAROLD. Why not? They're like Siamese Twins – them two. Pick them up together and then split them apart. It'll interfere with their telepathy, right? (*A huge vicious smile.*) Has anyone seen the major recently?

RAZORS. I heard he's a sick man. Bed-ridden.

HAROLD. Well, then, this'll make a nice change for him – a night out. You lot know who else. Arm up, get going and use the butchers' firm's trucks. And

me and Razors'll take a little ride to the Elephant and Castle.

The men clear the table of the fire arms.

ALAN. Where do we meet?

Everyone looks at Harold as they fondle the guns.

HAROLD. Two hours from now at the abattoir.

They begin to leave the gaming-room noisily and Harold stops them with a whistle. They look at him.

Remember, lads. Scare the shit out of them but don't damage them. I want them in the abattoir conscious and talkative – and another thing . . . try to be discreet, eh?

Harold turns away and checks his own automatic as the gang leaves. Just him and Jeff – Harold having indicated with a flick of his head that Razors should fetch the Jaguar. Jeff seems shaky. He gingerly fingers the remaining gun and Harold watches him drop it from his shaking hand.

HAROLD. I think we'd be employing your talents better if you went to help Victoria with the Yanks.

JEFF. If you're sure.

HAROLD. Oh, yeah . . . Do you reckon . . . Colin was jealous of you?

JEFF. Come again? (*A little unsure so he smiles.*)

HAROLD. Well . . . I was trying to ease him out. You know how potty he could go . . .

JEFF. So?

HAROLD. Well, is Colin the reason for all this? You know how bitchy queers get when their looks start fading . . .

JEFF. I don't know . . . Wasn't my type.

HAROLD. How do you stay so cool?

JEFF. I'm on the winning side.

HAROLD. Yeah. Help Vicky out, right?

But I want you at the abattoir at midnight, right?

JEFF. All right.

Harold watches Jeff go and then loads his automatic. He looks at Razors who has been watching, but is silent in the shadows.

7. Interior. Justine's. Night.

A very plush club/restaurant with a fashionable nouveau-riche clientele. We see Victoria, Charlie, Tony and Harris being shown to their table.

VICTORIA. Thank you.

WAITER. I didn't know Mr Shand wanted this table tonight.

VICTORIA. Yes, well, there was a change of plan.

CHARLIE. You can say that again.

WAITER. Would you care for a drink before you order?

VICTORIA. Charlie?

CHARLIE. Bourbon on the rocks.

TONY. I'll have the same, please.

HARRIS. Screwdriver, lots of vodka.

VICTORIA. San Bellagrino for me, please.

CHARLIE. I think we should skip the flambé cooking considering the gas situation in London.

VICTORIA. That sort of thing doesn't happen twice in one day.

CHARLIE. You should level with us. We're not just a pair of jerks out of college you know.

VICTORIA. No, absolutely not.

CHARLIE. Two bombs . . . that affects everyone . . .

HARRIS. Let's order, shall we? Er . . . *soupe du jour* and chef's special.

VICTORIA. Oh, I'll have my usual.

CHARLIE. No soup, hors d'oeuvres and the special.

TONY. I'll have the same.

VICTORIA. So. Charlie. How did you know about the bombs?

TONY. It's our business to know these things.

HARRIS. And, Ricardo – a bottle of champagne, very cold.

CHARLIE. Harold has got bad problems.

VICTORIA. But he's dealing with them, right now.

CHARLIE. He's been dealing with them all day.

VICTORIA. He's very thorough.

CHARLIE. I like your loyalty.

VICTORIA. I'm being frank.

CHARLIE. Victoria, unless you tell us what Harold's bad problems are and how he's dealing with them, I'm going to tell you what we're going to do. Tony and me, we're going to leave the table, we're going to check out of the Savoy – grab the first plane home. There'll be no deal.

TONY. It's not a good idea to bullshit us, Victoria.

VICTORIA. Cheers.

They all raise their glasses and drink.

CHARLIE. Well?

VICTORIA. A car was blown up . . . then a bomb was found at the Mayfair casino – it hadn't detonated. One of our men was found dead in a swimming pool –

HARRIS. Yeah, he was stabbed.

VICTORIA. I'm giving Charlie all the essential details.

HARRIS. I think that is an essential detail. (*He finishes his drink in a vulgar gulp.*)

CHARLIE. Auto . . . casino . . . stabbing . . . a bar blowing up. What is this, a gang war?

VICTORIA. No, no question of that.

CHARLIE. Then what?

VICTORIA. Isn't it obvious, Charlie? This deal is very big, some one is envious. Harold and I have no doubt that by tomorrow the problem will be settled.

TONY. You sound very confident.

VICTORIA. I am.

CHARLIE. Tony, you're the lawyer. Tell me what you think.

TONY. I think we can afford to give you 24 hours to resolve your problems before we make our final decision.

CHARLIE. Okay, Victoria, I'll give you 'til tomorrow. But just one more foul-up — and we're on our way back home.

VICTORIA. That goes without saying.

She smiles her 'winning' smile.

TONY. Nothing personal, Victoria, but business is business.

VICTORIA. I understand.

68. Interior. Elephant & Castle pub. Night.

A very crowded bar. A live band playing recent hits. We pick out two men at the bar with a couple of girls. All laughing. We see Harold enter and stand further along the bar. Jimmy spots him and signals to Billy. Both men go over to Harold somewhat apprehensively. Bill is a lot older than Jimmy.

BILLY. Harold! What are you doing this side of the river? You're straying a bit, aren't you?

HAROLD. How are you going, Billy, all right?

BILLY. Scotch?

JIMMY. Sorry to hear about your mother.

HAROLD. What's that?

JIMMY. Car blew up, didn't it? Well, that's what I heard . . .

BILLY. What's up, Harold — you got a spot of bother?

HAROLD. No, no, nothing. Loud in her ain't it?

BILLY. Oh, I'll get them to turn it down . . .

HAROLD. No, no. Listen, Billy. I've got a little bit of business I want to drop your way. Can we talk in the other bar?

BILLY. Right. Jimmy, bring the drinks round the back.

69. Exterior. Elephant & Castle pub. Night.

Billy and Harold leave the pub to walk to the other bar. We can still hear the music from inside. The street is empty.

BILLY. I heard about this American number, Harold. If there's anything going, put me in.

HAROLD. Well, the thing is, Billy, there's plenty of money for everybody. I just need the right people, know what I mean?

BILLY. Well, I'm your man, you know —

Razors materialises out of the darkness behind Billy and grabs him by the throat. Then he smashes Billy's bald head against the brick wall. Billy slumps as blood seeps down his face. Harold rams his hand in his overcoat pocket then prods Billy's back.

HAROLD. Walk to the car, Billy, or I'll blow your spine off.

BILLY. That's not a shooter, is it, Harold?

HAROLD. Oh, don't be silly, Billy. Would I come hunting for you with me fingers?

For the first and only time, Razors smiles as they get into the Jaguar.

'Don't treat me like one of your thugs, Harold,' says his mistress, Victoria.

'This is the work of some maniac. I'll have his carcass dripping blood by midnight,' says Harold, outraged to arrive at his favourite pub as it explodes.

'That was meant for me,' says Harold, surveying the debris and comforting a victim of the pub bombing. 'If we'd been here five minutes earlier . . .' says Victoria.

'Right lads, it's your decision – frostbite or verbals,' Harold tells the suspects he has rounded up as they hang from meathooks in the abattoir.

'Two or three Micks have been very busy covering a lot of ground since yesterday. It is impossible that no one knows nothing. Someone, somewhere knows.' Flanked by Jeff and Razors in his Mayfair casino, Harold instructs his gang to arm up.

'I heard you're having a spot of bother,' the South London gang boss tells Harold, surprised to find him south of the Thames. 'Let's go somewhere quiet for a little talk,' says Harold.

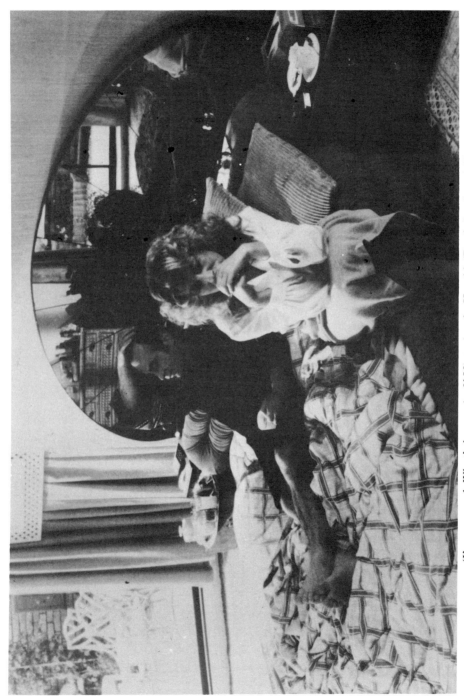

'I'm so scared. What's happening?' Victoria asks Harold. 'Don't let them kill us.'

70. Interior. Justine's. Night.

The meal is now at the coffee and cognac stage and Harris is disturbingly drunk, to Victoria's concealed disgust. Charlie and Tony evidently find the councillor tiresome.

HARRIS. It's all going to happen — with or without Harold. My hotels are going to be *there*.

CHARLIE. Will you get us a cab to the Savoy?

HARRIS. You see them, you see them, I'll show you the plans tomorrow. Magnificent. Pie in the sky hotels — well, you know what I mean. Something to be proud of.

VICTORIA. Yes, well, I think it's time we all went home, don't you?

HARRIS. No, no, come on, Victoria. Charlie understands. You understand, don't you, Charlie? We're two of a kind, me and him. We've had to crawl our way up from the gutter — we're self-made men. Right, Charles?

VICTORIA. I don't think Mr Restivo is as familiar with the gutter as you assume. (*She reaches down for her bag and quietly warns Harris.*) And if you don't watch your fucking step, councillor, you'll be right back in it.

HARRIS. Now, come on, Vicky, don't be like that. I'll tell you what — we'll have some more brandies at the bar, eh? I'll tell you all about my plans, Charlie.

They leave the table and approach the cocktail bar area next to the cloakrooms.

71. Interior. Cocktail bar. Night.

Harris is trying to wrap an arm around Victoria's waist. She pushes him away, almost knocking him off balance.

HARRIS. Now, now! Don't be hostile, Vicky.

Jeff is standing on the raised cocktail bar patio. Victoria is obviously very relieved to see him. She kisses his cheek briefly.

VICTORIA. Jeff! Am I glad you're here!

HARRIS (*slapping Jeff's face in a matey way*). Hello, son.

Jeff smiles at the Americans.

JEFF. Charlie, Tony — nice meal, everything all right?

CHARLIE. You tell me if everything's all right.

Victoria closes her eyes and then calmly faces Jeff.

VICTORIA. I've put our American friends in the picture about today.

JEFF. So you'll understand, Charlie, why Harold couldn't make it here. But everything is under control.

HARRIS. Oh yerrs. I'm sure the great Harold Shand'll find a way out of this one. Meanwhile, I'm going for a piss. Stay right where you are, Charlie —

Harris lurches off towards the lavatories.

CHARLIE. That guy is a loud mouth.

TONY. I don't like lushes. I don't like drunks. (*To Jeff.*) Do you trust him?

JEFF (*he swallows*). Harold can handle him. At the moment, that councillor is a very wise investment.

TONY. We'll talk about that tomorrow. Goodnight, Victoria.

He kisses her cheek very passingly and Charlie shakes her hand.

CHARLIE. Goodnight. Thanks for the dinner.

VICTORIA. Goodnight, Charlie.

JEFF. Goodnight.

When Charlie and Tony have taken their coats and gone:

VICTORIA. I really am so pleased to see

you, Jeff. That bloody Harris is a liability.

Jeff looks across the cocktail crowd to the bar where Harris is ordering another round of drinks with abandon.

What news?

JEFF. None yet.

Harris arrives with one large cognac for himself. He is in euphoric mood.

HARRIS. Where's the Yanks then? A waiter's coming with more brandies.

VICTORIA. Go home, Harris. Go home.

HARRIS. Don't sneer at me, Victoria. Don't look down your nose at me. It makes you go cross-eyed. You can't even see that I'm not the real bastard — he is.

Harris points his glass at Jeff and cognac splashes from it. But Victoria has gone to get her stole.

JEFF. I'll get you a cab home, councillor. And I'll talk to you later.

HARRIS. Okay. (*He drains his drink.*) Bastard.

72. Exterior. St Paul's Cathedral. Night.

Victoria drives the open-topped Mercedes through the empty streets towards the Barbican, her hair blowing and Jeff beside her.

VICTORIA. I don't think I've ever been so pleased to see anyone in my life. It was such a hard night.

She smiles at Jeff as the car rounds the Cathedral, its dome illuminated by floodlights against the night sky.

JEFF. You did a good job.

VICTORIA. Without the help of Councillor Harris.

JEFF. He fancies you. (*He looks at her body.*) But then so do a lot of people.

VICTORIA (*she laughs and accelerates*). It must be my 'sparkling' personality.

73. Exterior. Penthouse. Night.

Victoria, followed by Jeff, leaves the parked Mercedes and goes into the tower-block through the vast glass doors which two uniformed night porters open.

74. Interior. Penthouse foyer. Night.

Jeff takes in the luxury of the foyer as Victoria rushes to the lift. She is surprised that he is still with her.

JEFF. I'll see you to your door. Just in case.

He steps into the lift with her.

VICTORIA. Thank you.

75. Interior. Lift. Night.

They stand leaning against opposite walls looking at each other.

It won't go unless you press the button.

He presses the penthouse button without taking his eyes off her.

JEFF. It's not moving.

Victoria stretches across Jeff to re-press the button: he inhales her scent but doesn't move. The lift doors swish closed.

VICTORIA. It's temperamental. (*She leans against the wall again as far away from Jeff as possible in this confined space.*) I hate lifts.

Silence. Jeff keeps staring at her. She is inspecting the ceiling now.

It gets really claustrophobic in here with a lot of people.

JEFF. It depends on the people.

She looks at him.

I'd like to lick every inch of you.

The lift doors suddenly open. Victoria smiles.

VICTORIA. Saved by the bell. Goodnight, Jeff.

She walks out of the lift without looking back at him. Jeff hesitates, wondering whether to follow her. Before he can reach a decision the lift doors close.

76. Interior. Abattoir. Night.

The refrigeration store-room of the abattoir. Through an aisle of suspended frozen carcasses, Harold and Razors come towards us, through the mist of the frozen air. When they come into close-up, we realise that the 'meat' hanging beside Harold's head is not a carcass at all – it is the Elephant and Castle villain Billy, his forehead bloody, suspended upside down from a meat hook. Harold passes him without reaction.

77. Interior. Abattoir freezer room. Night.

Colin's corpse frozen in ice in a deep freezer – he still wears his swimming trunks. Harold stares at his body.

HAROLD. It's a long time since I've been to a funeral.

RAZORS. That's a strange thing, H. Did Jeff mention to you that funeral the day you got back from America?

Harold doesn't seem to be listening. He stares at Colin's ice shrouded head.

HAROLD. There used to be a funeral every half hour down the East India Dock Road . . .

RAZORS. A woman got out of the funeral car and gobbed at Jeff.

Harold turns slowly and frowns at Razors.

HAROLD. A?

RAZORS. I didn't see properly, I didn't crack on at the time –

The sound of the raucous arrival of Harold's men halts the conversation: shouts, yells and screams and the banging of doors.

78. Interior. Abattoir yard. Night.

From a fleet of butchers' trucks, Harold's men manoeuver the suspects they have collected onto the abattoir's meat hooks – bound and hanging upside down. They are shoved along the conveyor system like dead cattle until they reach the main area of the abattoir.

79. Interior. Abattoir. Night.

In a line the upside-down captives swing from the meat hooks high above Harold: one wears pyjamas, the others are too scared and confused to continue screaming.
Harold's men gather around him as he addresses the captives.

HAROLD. Everyone shut up.

His men stop their yells and taunts. A long silence as Harold paces the row of captives.

For more than ten years there's been peace. Everyone to his own patch. We've all had it sweet. I've done every single one of you favours in the past. (*A great bellow.*) I've treated the lot of you well. Even when you was out of order, right? Now there's been an eruption. Like fucking Belfast on a bad night.

At the far end of the abattoir, we can see Jeff who has suddenly arrived, shivering in the cold.

One of my dearest, closest friends is lying out there in a freezer and believe me, all of you – not one of you goes home until I find out who done it. And why?

Billy shakes on the hook until he is facing Harold, his face scarlet and one eye closed with dried blood from his forehead wound.

BILLY. Harold, listen, believe me – if I knew I'd say. The last thing I want is trouble with you. Everything's going too well for all of us.

*Jeff runs towards Billy and
unexpectedly starts punching him.*

EFF. You lying bastard.

BILLY. Things have never been so good
between South London and the East
End —

JEFF. Bastard, you fucking bastard.

HAROLD. Alan, you — get him off.

*Alan and Razors haul Jeff away from
Billy who is whimpering.
Harold grabs Jeff by his collar and
leads him towards the exit. Jeff still
wants to fight.*

Behave yourself boy, behave yourself.
You kill him and we've got gang war
on our hands, right?

JEFF. We already have — they're walking
all over you.

HAROLD. That's because we've got no
leads.

*From the doorway, Harold points at
the captives who are all staring at him.*

Right lads, it's your decision — frostbite or verbals. One of the two, right?

*The captives swing like conkers on
strings in the ventilated frosty air as a
security door outside slams with a
thud that echoes around the abattoir.*

80. Interior. Abattoir loading bay. Night.

*Parky has banged the door as he stands
and faces the agitated Harold. Jeff
watches from the doorway to the main
area.*

Parky! About time. Well?

PARKY. You've got to drop it, Harold.
It's not that lot. I've had the bomb
checked.

HAROLD. And?

PARKY. It's the same sort of device the
IRA use. This is Special Branch now,
Harold. I'm turning it over to them.

HAROLD. What the Irish got to do with
me? Just a bunch of hoods trying to
muscle in.

PARKY. For Christ's sake, Harold,
they're not just gangsters, they run
half of Londonderry on terror. Could
be London next.

HAROLD. Oh, no. I run London.

PARKY. Not now, Harold . . . they're
taking it away from you. It's Special
Branch and I'm getting out.

*Parky turns to walk away but Harold
halts him with a right hook. Parky
steadies himself and clutches his jaw.
Now he looks scared.*

HAROLD. Remember who pays your
wages, Parky. You ain't going
nowhere. Now — tell me something
worthwhile.

*We are aware that behind Harold
Jeff, Alan and Razors are watching.*

PARKY. There was a robbery at
Councillor Harris's demolition yard.
Explosives. We pulled in the security
guard — chappie called Flynn.

*Jeff's face for an instant registering
this.*

We grilled him for hours. He knew
something but he wouldn't say
anything. He was too scared.

Harold strides towards Alan.

HAROLD. Alan, you check out this
geezer Flynn. We'll make him talk.
Bring him in.

Alan nods.

PARKY. Harold, you can't do that!
(*Utterly desperate.*)

*Harold grabs Parky's jaw and shouts
into his face.*

HAROLD. Don't you tell me what I can
and can't do. Bent lawmen can be
tolerated only for so long as they are
lubricating and you have become
decidedly parched. If I was you Parky,
I'd run for cover and close the hatch.
'Cause you might well wind up on
one of those meat hooks, my son.

Harold patronisingly pats Parky's cheek and lets him go out of the abattoir.

All the gang are watching from the doorway. Harold instructs Jeff and Razors.

That lot in there, let them go. They don't know nothing. Jeff, you sort them out — clean them up and get them transport home. Give them a couple of grand each expenses, just keep them sweet, you know.

JEFF. What are you going to do now?

HAROLD. I'm going home. I need some time to think. But Alan, first thing tomorrow morning — bring that security guard in, right? Come on Razors, son. Drive me home.

As Harold and Razors go towards the exit Jeff bangs the door to get the men's attention.

JEFF. Get them at it, Dave — put the lot of them in a bubble bath and send them home.

81. Interior. Penthouse. Night.

The reflection of Victoria, waiting for Harold, on the wall of windows overlooking London's skyline. The apartment is luxurious. Victoria sits smoking jerkily on a sofa. She turns to face Harold who comes in quietly. He places his automatic on the bar beside the door and pours himself a hefty scotch in a crystal goblet.

HAROLD. How did it go with Charlie?

VICTORIA. Well . . . I stopped them going home.

Harold spins round and glares at her.

HAROLD. Going home?

VICTORIA. Yeah, they were going home — they're not stupid; they knew it was a bomb . . . and now they know the rest.

HAROLD. How?

VICTORIA. I told them.

HAROLD. You did what? (*Incredulous.*)

VICTORIA. I told them everything — Harold, I had to.

HAROLD. Victoria, listen, sweetheart. I'm setting up the biggest deal in Europe, with the hardest organisation since Hitler stuck a swastika on his jock-strap. I've been to incredible lengths to keep it incognito and now you, over a sherry, calmly tell the whole story?

VICTORIA. I had to tell them everything or the deal would have been finished. Harold, your trouble is, you just don't understand their psychology.

HAROLD. Bollocks, you smart-arsed pratt.

VICTORIA. . . . . I can't talk to you. I'm going to bed — goodnight.

Harold grabs Victoria as she stands to walk away, and throws her back onto the couch.

HAROLD. Oi, come here, I'm talking to you.

VICTORIA. Don't treat me like one of your thugs.

Victoria begins to sob quietly. Harold slumps beside her then hugs her anxiously.

HAROLD. What's happening to me? . . . I'm sorry. For ten years, it's been calm, no trouble . . . now this. Listen, I wouldn't hurt you for the world, I'm sorry.

VICTORIA. I'm so scared, Harold, I don't want to die. Don't let them kill us, Harold.

He kisses the top of her head.

HAROLD. It's all right, it's all right, we'll be all right, believe me.

Harold's face up close. For the first time, he looks scared as he hugs the weeping Victoria.

82. Exterior. Demolition yard. Day.

Pop music plays from a tinny transistor as we open on a warehouse through the metal wash of the yard's fence: a sign on a shed which reads: 'DANGER EXPLOSIVE'. We move into the shed which is stacked with boxes of explosives arranged on shelves protected by electric alarm wires.

Looking out through a window we see the arrival of a young housewife, hurrying from the old car she's just parked outside the gates. She shakes the gates and to her surprise finds the padlock broken. An Alsatian dog barks furiously then dashes to greet her as she comes into the yard. She peers into the security hut beside the gates. The door is open but the shed is empty. From here the transistor radio plays. The Alsatian knows her: it tries to get her to follow it into the warehouse. She looks up at the warehouse and slowly walks towards it. The dog is barking at the open door, wanting her to follow it inside.

83. Interior. Warehouse. Day.

In the darkness, the housewife follows the Alsatian up the creaking stairs nervously.

84. Exterior. Demolition yard. Day.

Looking down from the top floor of the warehouse, we see Alan get out of the car he has just parked. He locks the door.

85. Interior. Warehouse. Day.

The Alsatian is barking at the top of the stairs on the next level. As the housewife's head rises above the level of the floor she stares in horror. From her point of view: we see the security guard Flynn, obviously her husband, groaning on his back in the centre of the empty floor. His arms and legs are outstretched.

86. Exterior. Demolition yard. Day.

Alan is strolling towards the yard when he hears Mrs Flynn's agonised screaming. He runs into the yard.

87. Interior. Warehouse. Day.

Mrs Flynn is kneeling beside her husband, sobbing. He has been crucified, nailed to the floor through his feet and palms. He is on the brink of death. The Alsatian is barking and running backwards and forwards as Alan breathlessly reaches the top floor. Alan closes his eyes at the gasping final breaths Flynn takes. His wife begins to whimper when she realises he has stopped breathing.

88. Interior. Penthouse bedroom. Day.

Harold and Victoria, wearing bath robes, lie side by side on the vast bed: behind them the open French windows lead onto the rooftop garden. At the foot of the bed stands Alan. He has just reported the death of Flynn the security guard.

ALAN. Well, I'm sorry, H.

HAROLD. It's all right, Alan, it's not your fault, you weren't to blame. There's some fresh coffee in the kitchen, go and make yourself some breakfast.

Alan leaves the room, closing the door. Harold lights a cigarette. He shares it with Victoria.

VICTORIA. So . . . someone got to him before you could. How did they know – or was it a coincidence?

HAROLD. Stretching it a bit, ain't it?

VICTORIA. That means it's someone close to home . . . You know, last night in the restaurant . . . funny feeling . . . Harris being really strange. He said that I'd got it all wrong, that Jeff was the real bastard. Why should he say that?

Harold ponders, then sits up and reaches for the phone. He jabs the buttons and waits as it rings.

HAROLD. Hello, Razors? That funeral you told me about. Some bird gobbing in Jeff's face . . . that's right! Well, find that woman, I want to talk to her. Well, get her name and address off the undertakers. Right, and as soon as you've found her, come and pick me up. Right, I'll see you.

Victoria watches Harold pace the room.

89. Exterior. Cemetery. Day.

The sun shines as a young woman arranges flowers on a new grave. Her two children play among the gravestones. She looks up as Harold approaches through the evergreens. She is Carol, and she has been crying.

CAROL. You're a bastard, Harold Shand. A vicious bastard. You deserted him and you left him to die in a stinking ditch and you didn't even have the decency to —

She is becoming hysterical and Harold slaps her cheek. The children rush to her and she hugs them. Silence.

HAROLD. When did he die?

CAROL. Ten days ago, you should know.

HAROLD. Where?

CAROL. Belfast.

HAROLD. Belfast? (*Incomprehension.*) What was he doing there?

CAROL. That Jeff of yours sent him.

HAROLD. Jeff?

CAROL. Hired him. He went with that blond one, that Colin. Always asked him to do the chauffeuring on the long runs.

HAROLD. A chauffeur?

CAROL. My Phil was a minicab driver.

HAROLD. Your husband drove my

Colin — and he got topped in Belfast?

CAROL. And abandoned there. I was left with all the arrangements. To bring the body back here, and the funeral and not so much as a penny for the kids . . .

They stare at Harold.

HAROLD. And Jeff hired him?

CAROL. And that bastard hasn't paid me any compensation.

She begins to sob again.

HAROLD. All right, all right. You'll get some compensation. The Corporation'll look after you. Is there anything you need?

CAROL. I need a hundred quid a week.

HAROLD. All right. You'll get it. Anything else?

CAROL. I just want him back.

She breaks down completely and falls on the grave. Harold can't cope with this. He looks away.

HAROLD. Get him a decent stone and send me the bill.

A wide view of the cemetery: flowers, trees, sunshine. Harold standing, not knowing what to do, beside the sobbing widow and her children.

90. Exterior. Yacht. Day.

Harold arrives in the Jaguar. It screeches to a halt at the gangplank and he climbs aboard.

91. Interior. Harold's study on the yacht. Day.

Harold watches through the slats of the window's blind as Jeff arrives in his Mercedes. Harold pours himself a tumblerful of scotch and sits at his desk waiting.

He looks up as Jeff comes in. Harold smiles and tosses the scotch bottle to Jeff who catches it.

HAROLD. Have a drink? (*He smiles.*)

JEFF. All right. (*He pours a large scotch.*)

HAROLD. You never worry about your liver?

JEFF. No, we're just good friends.

HAROLD. When my mum used to have a go at my old man about his boozing, he always used to say 'If you drink less than your doctor, you're all right.'

JEFF. It's hot in here — shall we go on deck?

HAROLD. Hot? . . .
You hot?
This'll cool you down.

Harold seats himself behind his desk.

JEFF. What do you want to talk about? . . . Shouldn't we be . . . well, all what's going on . . .

HAROLD. Everything's all right.

JEFF. All right?

HAROLD. I'm using the word the way you use it.

JEFF. What . . . 'all right'? (*Jeff sits down. He is ill at ease.*)

HAROLD. Well. I remember vividly when you met me at Heathrow, off the plane from New York, I said 'How's things been' and you said . . . 'All right.'

JEFF. I'm not with you.

HAROLD. Ain't you? Top up?

Harold slides the bottle across the desk towards Jeff who slowly gets up from the couch and collects it. He looks wearily at Harold who sits in shadow — just a shaft of sunlight through the venetian blind makes a stripe across his eyes. It is as if Jeff can only see Harold's eyes.

HAROLD. Quite frankly Jeff, I'm a bit flabbergasted you forgot to mention this carry-on what happened in Belfast when I was away.

Jeff gulps a mouthful from his glass and now his voice is strained.

JEFF. Oh, that . . .

HAROLD. Yeah . . . that. What about this minicab driver, Phil Benson?

JEFF. He's . . . well, he was . . . a friend of Colin's. Got killed . . . it's a long story . . . I know, I should have told you —

HAROLD. Well, tell me now! What the bloody hell was Colin doing with a Limehouse minicab driver in Belfast?

JEFF. Colin can't drive.

HAROLD. Oh, that makes sense. Second question — Belfast. What was he doing there? I know Colin fancied soldiers, but that's taking his buggering a bit far, ain't it?

JEFF. He had to make a delivery.

HAROLD. Well — a delivery of what? Well, come on, I'm curious. Chieftain tanks? Bars of chocolate? Fiesta Durex — what?

JEFF. Money.

HAROLD. Ain't they got any banks out there? Well, what money — what for and who to?

JEFF. He was delivering for Harris. He had a problem. He was being leant on to deliver — to deliver money, I mean, to Belfast.

HAROLD. Leant on by who?

JEFF. He's got a hundred Micks on his labour force. He's out of business without them. He was being leaned on to organise the delivery. He asked me.

HAROLD. So you got my Colin . . . to deliver for Harris . . . money to Belfast?

JEFF. Yeah.

HAROLD. Well, that is irregular. I . . . don't approve of my men delivering funds for the IRA.

Harold's face looks murderous. Jeff seems to sway for a moment.

JEFF. He had no choice. He has to do what they ask. Otherwise his buildings don't get built. That's why he never has a strike — that's why we use Harris.

Harold walks to the bar with his back to Jeff. Then he punches it savagely.

HAROLD. Jesus Christ. Of all the faces you could have used, of all of them — you pick Colin for a job like that! (*Now he faces Jeff and shakes his head at the realisation.*) So he took a dip, eh?

JEFF. Yeah. He stupidly helped himself.

HAROLD. How much?

JEFF. Five grand.

Harold's astonished reaction.

HAROLD. Do what? You mean all this anarchy is over five poxy grand?

JEFF. And three of their top men were wiped out. On the night Colin delivered.

HAROLD. So, they've put two and two together and they've come up with the answer, ain't they? As Colin's my man, it's down to me. I'm the one that's grassed them up, ain't I? This is all revenge!

JEFF. Yeah . . .

HAROLD. Revenge! Fucking show them! That security guard . . . Flynn . . . he could give us a clue, couldn't he?

JEFF. Does he say anything? (*Very nervous.*)

HAROLD. No . . . not much when Alan got to him.

JEFF. No?

HAROLD. No. Alan found him dying. He'd been nailed to the floor.

JEFF. When was this then?

HAROLD. Well, it must have been just after you saw him and before Alan

saw him. Otherwise, you would have noticed wouldn't you? I mean, a geezer nailed to the floor . . . a man of your education would definitely have spotted that.

Jeff tries to back away.

JEFF. Now look!

Harold pounces on him, knocking Jeff to the floor. Harold has Jeff by the hair and neck pinned against the wall.

HAROLD. You fucking Judas!

JEFF. I didn't *do* anything.

HAROLD. Maybe you didn't nail the geezer but it's down to you all the same, ain't it.

JEFF. Nothing to do with me.

HAROLD. Don't lie to me, boy. I can smell your lies and I can smell something else. I can smell your greed and ambition and something more disgusting — betrayal. Why, Jeff, why?

JEFF (*like a child*). They threatened to kill me. I was scared.

Jeff's eyes pleading with Harold. Harold unexpectedly releases Jeff and staggers to the bar.

HAROLD. You put the finger on me, didn't you?

JEFF. I didn't . . . it was Harris.

HAROLD. For Micks! Pig-eyed Micks! Red-necked terrorist scum.

JEFF. Don't blame me, blame Colin —

HAROLD. Revenge! (*Shouting, more to himself than to Jeff.*) It's me that's going to take revenge. I'll crush them like beetles.

JEFF (*a note of scorn*). Never.

HAROLD. I'm going to annihilate them!

JEFF. You can't wipe them out —

HAROLD. You just watch me boy!

JEFF. Kill ten, twenty — bring out the tanks and the flame throwers . . . They'll just pour back. Like an army of ants. (*Face to face with Harold now*.) Work with them.

HAROLD. It's my manor. (*He reaches for the bottle again*.)

JEFF. Jesus Christ, the British Army's been diving about with shit flying at them for the last ten years and you're not impressed —

HAROLD. Shut up.

JEFF. They can take over here anytime they want.

HAROLD. I said, shut up.

JEFF (*now shouting*). You won't stop them. To them you're nothing — nothing. The shit on their shoes, the —

Harold swings round with the bottle and smashes it across Jeff's skull. Harold sits astride Jeff's chest and frenziedly thrusts the jagged edge of the bottle into his throat again and again.

HAROLD. You bastard, you bastard.

Harold begins to freeze as blood spurts from Jeff's neck. He drops the bottle and embraces the trembling body until it becomes motionless.
Harold's face up close as he releases the body. His shirt front is smothered with Jeff's blood.

92. Exterior. yacht. Day.

Victoria is getting out of the Cortina driven by Alan when a terrifying scream vibrates from the yacht and she looks up to see Harold staggering down the gangplank, blood over his face and hands as well as clothes. He is demented. Razors runs towards the yacht from the Jaguar. Victoria and Alan stare at Harold as he lurches to the quay.

HAROLD. Jeff . . . and Harris, done me over. I'm going to kill him. Razors, get me that fucking gun —

Harold runs towards the Jaguar pushing away Alan who tries to hold him. Victoria gets between the car and

Harold and wallops him with both hands until Harold calms down. He stands breathing deeply. Victoria grips his wrists and speaks to him as though he's retarded.

VICTORIA. Now you've got Harris, right? You've got him, so use him.

Harold is staring at her. She shakes him.

Use him to stop this bloody havoc.

Harold slumps into the back seat of the Jaguar and rests his head on Victoria's breasts when she sits beside him. Razors gently drives the Jaguar away from the yacht as Victoria strokes Harold's head.

93. Interior. Penthouse bathroom. Day.

Harold stands naked under the shower caressing himself as much as washing away the blood stains. There is clotted blood in his hair and between his teeth: the water at his feet is red. This is like an exorcism.

94. Exterior. Penthouse roof garden. Day.

Victoria and Razors burn Harold's blood stained clothes on the roof garden barbecue. She watches the clothing burn and vanish in the flames.

95. Interior. Penthouse bedroom. Day.

Harold has dressed and Victoria fixes his cuff links. He puts on his jacket and looks calm and utterly in control of himself. He follows Razors to the door.

96. Interior. Town Hall foyer. Day.

A late middle-aged, uniformed commissionaire greets Harold and Razors as they stride into the foyer. Victorian marbled splendour.

HAROLD. Councillor Harris's office, please.

COMMISSIONAIRE. Yes sir. I'll show you the way.

They climb the wide stairway.

COMMISSIONAIRE. He's on the second floor.

HAROLD. Terrific.

Harold is carrying an executive briefcase. He looks at it.

97. Interior. Town Hall balcony. Day.

They reach the balcony which overlooks the foyer.

COMMISSIONAIRE. Friend of yours, sir?

HAROLD. Very old friend, yes.

COMMISSIONAIRE. Nice man, Councillor Harris. And a bloody hard worker. He's been on that phone all morning.

HAROLD. Is that so? I hear he does a lot for the Irish community around here.

COMMISSIONAIRE. So they tell me. (*He pauses to peer into the glass-boxed, open book of remembrance.*) It's three weeks since they turned the pages of the Book of Remembrance.

HAROLD. Really?

COMMISSIONAIRE. There's a work to rule.

They continue to climb the stairs.

I said to the union bloke, I said 'It's a good job they didn't work to rule in the trenches in France in 14-18.'

98. Interior. Town Hall corridor. Day.

They halt outside a door. The building seems to be deserted.

HAROLD. This is it?

COMMISSIONAIRE. The very same. Are you going to need me to show you the way down?

HAROLD. I think I can manage that.

Thank you.

The Commissionaire smiles and walks away down the corridor to the staircase.
When he is out of sight, Harold briskly bangs his knuckles on the door and opens it, while Razors feels for the gun in his inside pocket. Harold strides into the office.

HARRIS VOICE. Harold? I didn't expect to see you.

99. Exterior. Stockcar stadium. Night.

A big stockcar race meeting in progress and an excited crowd. Through the crowd we pick out Harris with Razors and Harold weaving their way towards the main stand.
As they reach it, Harris glances up at the office window overlooking the race track. Razors, using the pocketed gun, nudges Harris towards the stairway leading to it.
At the foot of the stairway Harris falters.

HARRIS. Harold, call it off. You can't do it. You can't deal with these people. For Christ's sake – they're not interested in money. They're political, they're idealists, they're fanatical –

RAZORS (*shoving Harris forward*). Come on, George.

As Harris reluctantly begins to climb the stairway, Harold turns to look across the stadium to a floodlight pylon. From his point of view we close in to see one of his men adjusting the sights of a rifle, pointed at the office window above Harold. Harold begins to climb.

100. Interior. Stadium office. Night.

O'Flaherty sits at desk by the window overlooking the track, eating from a meal set on a tray. He pours from a half bottle of champagne and sips his drink as Harris enters. O'Flaherty slowly turns and looks at Harold who stands beside Harris holding the briefcase in both hands.

HARRIS. This is Harold Shand.

HAROLD. There's sixty grand in here. To make sure there's no more aggro.

He puts the briefcase on the desk and opens it to reveal the stacks of bank notes.

O'FLAHERTY. You'll have to wait to see the boss about that.

HAROLD. Where is he?

O'Flaherty nods towards the window.

O'FLAHERTY. There . . . he's just won the last race.

Harold looks out of the window.
From his point of view we see the boss being driven into the pits below, accepting the cheers of the crowd, holding the trophy he's just received above his head. He looks up at Harold.
Harold turns away from the window and paces the office. Harris is shaking in a corner. O'Flaherty continues to sip the champagne and pick at his meal.
Harold glances quickly to the sniper's position then paces towards Harris, intimidating him to move towards the desk right in front of the window.
The boss comes in and puts his crash-helmet on a chair beside the door. He looks at Harris then Harold. Harold moves out of the sniper's view through the window.

O'FLAHERTY. This is Mister Shand. He's brought the money and he wants an answer.

The boss glances at the open briefcase then looks at Harold.

BOSS. How much is there?

HAROLD. Sixty grand. You'd better count it.

BOSS. If you don't mind, I will.

He walks to the desk and he and

O'Flaherty begin to count the stacks of bank notes. Harold is beside the door and quickly flings it open. Razors is standing there and fires several times at the boss as the sniper also opens fire.*
Harris is caught in the cross fire as the boss and O'Flaherty both fall to the ground. Harris staggers backwards and smashes through the window.

101. Exterior. Stadium office. Night.

Harris smashes onto a car as it passes beneath the window and the car skids, causing a pile-up of the cars behind it. One bursts into flames.

102. Exterior. Savoy Hotel. Night.

Harold's Jaguar stops outside the Strand entrance of the hotel and he bounces out in happy mood. Victoria smiles from the back seat.

HAROLD. Wait there while I go and get them. All right?

She kisses Harold as Razors switches off the engine.

103. Exterior. Savoy Hotel foyer. Night.

Harold at the reception desk.

HAROLD. Mister Restivo's suite, please.

RECEPTIONIST. Suite 513.

Harold strides towards the lifts.

104. Interior. Hotel bedroom. Night.

Tony is strapping up his suitcase when Harold opens the door and enters triumphantly.

HAROLD. Where's Charlie?

Harold notices the packed suitcases and frowns. Charlie comes in from next room. Harold is euphoric.

HAROLD. Everything's all right! All the troubles are over!

Charlie looks at Tony in disbelief..

CHARLIE. What did he say? Sorry, Harold, but I'm glad you dropped in to say goodbye. That's real nice.

HAROLD. What — you leaving?

CHARLIE. Yeah.

HAROLD. What — you're not going back to New York?

TONY. Next flight out.

HAROLD. Here, come on, Charlie, I know we've had a few problems but you've only been here a couple of days —

CHARLIE. Yeah, a couple of days that turned out to be another St Valentine's Day massacre.

HAROLD. But I've settled it . . . once and for all.

TONY (*on the phone*). Yes, I'd like a porter to suite five thirteen, please. And we'd like a cab right away. (*He replaces the receiver.*)

HAROLD. You two can't wait to get out of here, can you?

CHARLIE. I always react that way to bombs blowing up. Mass murders. It's a hang-up of mine.

HAROLD. It's coming to something when the Mafia can't handle a little problem, ain't it? (*He laughs derisively.*)

CHARLIE. Tony, did you hear what he said? 'A little problem'! Harold, this is like a bad night in Vietnam.

HAROLD. But it's over — I pulled the plug on them.

TONY. We do not deal with gangsters, period. This country's a worse risk than Cuba was. It's a banana republic. You're a mess.

CHARLIE. Ciao, Harold.

Tony continues to strap up his suitcase and Charlie locks his briefcase. They both have their backs to Harold who hesitates before going to the door. He opens it, then smiles.

HAROLD. Well . . . bon voyage, then.

Charlie and Tony smile at Harold.

HAROLD. I'll tell you something . . . I'm glad I found out in time just what a partnership with a pair of wankers like you would have been. A sleeping partner's one thing, but you're in a fucking coma! No wonder you've got an energy crisis your side of the water. Us British . . . we're used to a bit more vitality . . . imagination . . . touch of the Dunkirk spirit — know what I mean? (*He points an accusing finger at them.*) The days when Yanks could come over here and buy up Nelson's Column and an Harley Street surgeon and a couple of Windmill girls are definitely over!

TONY. Now, look —

HAROLD. Shut up, you long streak of paralysed piss. What I'm looking for is someone who can contribute to what England has given to the world . . . Culture . . . sophistication . . . genius . . . A little bit more than an hot dog — know what I mean?

We're in the Common Market now and my new deal is with Europe. I'm going into partnership with a German organisation — Yeah, the Krauts! They've got ambition . . . know-how . . . and they don't lose their bottle.

Look at you . . . the Mafia? I shit 'em.

He goes out laughing, leaving the door open.

105. Exterior. Savoy Hotel. Night.

Harold gets into the rear of Jaguar. As it suddenly shoots forward he realises he's alone in the back seat.

HAROLD. Here, hold up — where's Victoria?

From his point of view we see Victoria in rear window of car ahead of the Jaguar — trapped between two men,

*her mouth gagged, a terrified look in
her eyes.*

106. Interior. Jaguar. Day.

*Harold looks ahead into the driver's
rear view mirror and to his horror sees
not Razor's eyes, but the smiling eyes of
the Irish Boss he thought had been shot.
From around the seat beside the driver
looms the grinning face of the pretty
boy who stabbed Colin in the swimming
baths. He has an automatic pointing at
Harold. The Jaguar proceeds along the
Strand.*